MY JASPER JUNE

ALSO BY LAUREL SNYDER

Orphan Island

Seven Stories Up

Bigger than a Bread Box

Penny Dreadful

Any Which Wall

Up and Down the Scratchy Mountains

LAUREL SNYDER

MY JASPER JUNE

WALDEN POND PRESS

An Imprint of HarperCollinsPublishers

Walden Pond Press is an imprint of HarperCollins Publishers.
Walden Pond Press and the skipping stone logo are trademarks and registered trademarks of Walden Media, LLC.

My Jasper June

www.harpercollinschildrens.com

ISBN 978-0-06-283662-5 (trade)
ISBN 978-0-06-295504-3 (special edition)

19 20 21 22 23 PC/LSCH 10 9 8 7 6 5 4 3 2 1
❖
First Edition

FOR CHRIS

There is a crack in everything.
That's how the light gets in.
—Leonard Cohen

THE LAST DAY

The heavy doors of the school swung open, and we all burst out into the heat, scattering across the lawn. It was like something had exploded inside the building and hurled us into summer. Kids shouted and laughed and shoved each other. Kids flooded the sidewalk. Kids spilled into the bright sunlight of late May in Atlanta and squinted. They threw things—wads of paper and hot Cheetos and candy wrappers. Someone screamed. Someone was singing. Someone hopped on a bike and tore off down Emerson. But mostly everyone hung around.

This is the last day of school, I thought to myself.

This is kids having fun on the last day of school.

If you're in a mood to laugh and shout, it's a good time. If you're not, it's really weird to just stand there, in the middle of all that noise, watching and listening.

This is me, on the last day of school.

"Heads up, Leah!" Someone yelled my name, and I turned as a Frisbee flew straight at my head. I ducked, and it just missed me, sailed on, and banged into a tree. I turned back around.

The other three girls standing near me had been talking all at once, really fast and happy since we stepped outside, but I hadn't been paying attention. It's funny how, when there's enough noise, you can sort of tune it all out, so that it blurs into a hum of sounds. But now Tess looked over and set a hand gently on my arm. "You okay?"

"Yeah, I'm fine," I said. "It's just . . ." I didn't know what to say. I never seemed to know anymore. "I guess I'm ready for vacation."

"I know, right?" she said, smiling. "We were all just talking about that." She looked at Lane and Minnah. They nodded.

"You're coming to Morelli's, yeah?" Minnah asked me. "For ice cream?"

"Of course she is!" said Tess, throwing an arm over my shoulder. "It's the last day of school, after all."

"Good!" said Lane. "It wouldn't feel right without Leah."

Then they all started talking again, and I tuned back out.

It was a tradition. The tradition of *Tess and Leah and Lane and Minnah.* The group of us walked home together after school every day, with a bunch of boys straggling behind us. Sometimes we talked to the boys and sometimes we didn't. And on the last day of school, every year, we shared a banana split at Morelli's.

Everything was a tradition in Ormewood Park.

The tradition of *Friday-night neighborhood parties*, with parents wandering loosely from house to house, beers in hand, and kids playing in the front yards.

The tradition of *five-alarm Halloween chili at the Minkewicz place*.

The tradition of *the Eden Avenue Sledding Hill and Winter Olympics*, on the rare occasion it snowed.

The tradition of *Leah and Tess are best friends, and always have been*.

New people who moved to Ormewood Park learned these traditions right away, because everyone was quick to share their stories. "Ormewood is a really special place," someone would usually say. "It's not like other neighborhoods in Atlanta. We're one big family, really."

And that was true.

But as I followed Tess's backpack down Woodland Avenue, along the familiar cracked sidewalks, I found myself thinking about how it might feel to live somewhere different. Where it wasn't always the same. Where you could go straight home, alone, on the last day of school, if you were feeling tired, no matter what the traditions were.

The truth was that, on the first last-day-of-school since last summer, it wasn't the same for me at all. It couldn't be. And the pretending was painful. Like I'd been carrying something very heavy for way too long and I just wanted to go home and set it down.

When we neared the ice cream shop, Lane and Minnah bolted ahead, and Tess followed them, turning to shout at me, "There's a massive line, come on!"

So I ran too. Because it didn't seem fair not to. *It wouldn't feel right without Leah.* But running gave me the funniest feeling. Like I was running with my feet, but my brain wasn't running. My heart wasn't running.

This is what Leah looks like when she runs, I thought to myself.

This is Leah running to join her friends for celebratory last-day-of-school ice cream. Just like always.

As we ate our banana split, everyone was full of summer plans. Lane was going to see her grandparents in Canada, and Minnah was visiting her family in Vietnam, and Tess was going to New York, like every summer. I listened to them talk and waited for what I knew had to come next. Sure enough, it did. Minnah turned to me, with a mouthful of fudge, and asked, "What about *you*, Leah? You going to camp like usual?"

I looked to Tess, and her eyes were wide, waiting to see what I'd say.

What could I say?

"No. I'm not really doing anything this summer."

"Oh," said Lane, looking a little uncomfortable. "Well, that's cool. Then you can just relax, right? And maybe there will be some great last-minute surprise thing. A road trip?"

I shook my head. "I don't think so," I said. "I don't think my parents are up for surprises this summer."

Then everyone was quiet for a minute, and we all peered down at our ice cream, scraped at the banana boat with our spoons, trying to find some last bit of goodness, even though it was really all gone.

Walking home from Morelli's, just the two of us, Tess and I didn't say much. What was there to say? I didn't belong the way I once had. I had been a part of something, a puzzle piece, and now it was like a bit of me had broken off and I didn't fit the puzzle anymore.

At my front walk, Tess stopped as I headed up the steps. Any other year, she'd have come in with me. We'd have hung out in my room, or maybe sat under the sprinkler. Probably she'd have stuck around for dinner, and then her parents would have ended up at our place, to grill some chicken. But it wasn't going to happen today, and we both knew it. I felt sad about that, but also I wanted her to go. It was almost like I was allergic to this, to her. It was hard trying to fake it. Trying to be okay for someone else.

"Well," said Tess. "I'll see you tomorrow, right? At the Zyskowskis' schoolwork burn?"

"I don't think so," I said, shaking my head. "I threw away almost everything at school. I don't have any papers left to toss in the bonfire."

"Really?" she said. "But it'll be the first time without you since kindergarten, and it's a tradition. . . ." Even as her voice trailed off, I could tell that Tess wasn't really surprised. Not anymore.

A few years ago, Tess's favorite necklace had broken off while we were tubing on the Chattahoochee River. There'd been no way to go back and get it. And I remembered watching her as she stared back at the churning water and the rocks, while our boat tumbled on forward into the next set of rapids. The river's current had been unstoppable, and Tess had seen that and accepted it. Her necklace was gone for good.

The look on Tess's face that day on the river had been the same one I stared at now. She and I stood there in front of my house, and it was like we were agreeing to something. Neither of us said a word, but I swear we were thinking the very same thought. Together. We were letting go. And we knew it.

Part of me wanted to change my mind, to not be thinking what I was thinking. Part of me loved Tess, and wanted to walk down the porch steps and hug her and make everything okay again. But I couldn't do it. The river's current was unstoppable. We had lost something precious, and we knew just where it was, but that didn't mean we could turn back for it.

Everything was *not* okay, and I was done pretending.

I shrugged. "Sorry."

"Well, then . . . see you around, I guess," said Tess.

"See you around," I said. And I waved goodbye, like in a movie. Like I was standing on a ship instead of my porch. Heading off on a long voyage.

Tess turned and walked off in the direction of her house. She didn't glance back, just kept walking.

And I watched her go. I waited until I couldn't see her anymore.

This is what it looks like when Leah says goodbye, I thought.

As it turned out, dinner that night was grilled chicken after all, but it came from Whole Foods in a cardboard box instead of the grill, and it was eaten inside, at the kitchen table. I'd spent all afternoon watching *Lord of the Rings* clips on my phone in my room and thinking about napping. So I'd barely registered when my parents came home, but suddenly there was a knock on my door and my mother's voice: "Leah! Dinner!"

I wasn't hungry, but dinnertime was a requirement, and if I didn't show up in the kitchen, I knew it would be a big deal. So I found myself sitting at the old yellow table, poking at reheated grilled chicken and some sort of herby couscous or quinoa. I could never remember which was which. We sat in silence—the three of us—chewing loudly in the white-tiled room.

After a little while, Dad cleared his throat, and I looked up at him. Throat clearing meant he wanted to say something but needed to be prompted. Sure enough, Mom fluttered, "What is it, babe?"

"I was just thinking," said Dad, staring at a piece of chicken on his fork, "if Leah isn't going to camp this year like usual, she should take a class. Shouldn't she? Or do something else? Something productive? Not just sit around?"

"Oh," said Mom. Her brow creased. "Oh . . . you're right, Paul. I don't know how I didn't think about it. I just didn't." She set down her water glass heavily.

"We've had a lot going on this year," said Dad.

"Yes, well," said Mom, waving away the excuse with a flick of her hand. "In any case, it slipped my mind. I wonder what's still open. What kind of thing were you thinking about? I can make some calls tomorrow, from work."

Dad shrugged. "I don't know. Don't they do something over at the zoo, with animals? I see lots of kids there whenever I drive past. It *looks* like a summer camp sort of thing. Or maybe she could learn coding?"

"Hmmm." Now Mom was chewing her thumbnail.

I just sat, waiting. Watching them. In silence.

Sometimes parents are like wild animals. If you don't make

any loud noises or sudden movements, they'll forget you're there and leave you be. I was pretty sure that Dad's *something at the zoo* was a day camp for little kids. Like a petting zoo with snack and nap time. And I did *not* want to spend the summer hunched over a computer, learning to code lame video games with a bunch of grubby ten-year-old boys. But I also didn't think I was going to help my case any by arguing with my parents, so I kept my mouth shut.

Now Mom had her phone out and was scrolling through it quickly. I wondered what exactly she'd googled.

Aimless thirteen-year-old activities

Last-minute summer camp ideas

Moms who screw up and forget about vacation

After a minute, she glanced up from the phone to stare at me. "What do you think, Leah? What would you be interested in? Soccer, maybe? Or you could volunteer somewhere? Theater? You used to like putting on little plays, didn't you? With Tess?"

I stuck a bite of chicken in my mouth and made a sound that might have been *I dunno* but also might have been *leave me alone.*

"The thing is," said Mom, turning back to Dad again, "even if we found something, how would we get her there? Who would drive, if we're both at work?" She looked at Dad. "Do you think *you* could manage to . . ."

Dad shook his head. "Maybe we could find something on the bus line?"

"Oh, Paul. Nobody actually takes the bus. But maybe . . . maybe she's old enough to be alone. I was babysitting at her age. Do you think you're ready for that, Leah?"

Before I could answer, Dad rose from his chair. "Hey, sorry," he said. "I know I started this up, but can we figure it out tomorrow? I need to get to darts."

"Darts" was the once-a-week dart game he played with some other dads on the block, in bars around town. *It was a tradition.*

"I guess—sure, that's fine," said Mom. She set her phone on the table and poked at whatever it was but didn't take a bite.

Watching her, I couldn't help thinking that Mom always needed something to do with her hands. She always needed something to hold. To fidget with. Why was that? Why couldn't she ever just *be*?

Dad gave a quick wave to no one in particular and turned to go. Mom raised her water glass to him as the kitchen door opened and closed. Then the room was quiet again.

I set my napkin on the table, closed my eyes, and exhaled in relief. I could see now that Dad's suggestion wasn't going anywhere at all. It was probably too late to sign me up for anything worth doing, and it's not like there was anything I wanted to do anyway. Dad was just trying to be a dad and Mom was just trying to be a mom. Even though neither of them could really remember how. In a few minutes Mom would wash the dishes and go turn on the TV or read a book. And then we could all stop pretending I was going to do anything more than nothing all summer.

A summer of nothing sounded exactly right to me.

ACTUAL PANTS

The next morning, I woke up to the sound of silence. There was none of the usual racket of songbirds, so I knew it must be late. I reached for my phone and checked the time: 10:27. I guessed that meant my parents had decided I *was* old enough to do nothing, all by myself.

I smiled and let my eyes fall shut again. Then I lay there, feeling the heaviness of my limbs on the bed, the sheet light and cool above my body. Feeling nothing. It was officially summer, and the only place I really wanted to be was here, in bed, half asleep. For days. Weeks. Months. In this bubble of fuzzy morning, with the sun up and slanting through the blinds. I could never remember my dreams these days—only the glow of not quite remembering. Only the vague shine of sleep.

I let myself drift back into it.

It was perfect. Exactly what I'd hoped for. I'd wake up each day in the yellow light of late morning, with dust motes floating over my eyes, and Mr. Face purring softly beside me. I'd pet him for a minute, then drift, dream, and fall back asleep. But finally, about noon, I'd get to that point where no matter how long I stayed in bed with my eyes closed, my brain wouldn't stop clicking, working, turning over, and wanting to get up.

Then I'd drag myself out of bed and change from pajama pants to leggings, so that if Mom came home for lunch unexpectedly or something, I'd look semi-dressed. After that I'd make something to eat—a Hot Pocket, maybe, or cheese and crackers. Then I'd go lie down on the couch, to watch movies on the TV—one day it was *My Neighbor Totoro*, another *A Wrinkle in Time*—or just flip around in my phone, staring at my classmates' pictures from vacation. From the looks of it, everyone was having an outrageously good time. Lots of grinning and shoulder posing and exotic Popsicles.

By late afternoon, my eyes would glaze over with what Mom called *phone brain*, so I'd switch to reading. Mostly books I'd read before, in elementary school. The kinds of books where regular kids had magical adventures in their own backyards. *Breadcrumbs, The Jumbies, The Seventh Wish.* I liked wishing books best of all. Books that made it seem like incredible things might happen to anyone.

And then, later, when I heard keys jangling in the door and Mom and Dad poked their heads in, I got good-kid points for the fact that I was reading on my own.

"Who says kids don't read anymore?" Dad might say.

"I *told* you she was mature enough to stay home alone," Mom might add. "Our Leah makes good decisions."

Then dinner would happen, and eventually bed. So that I could fall asleep and start all over again the next day.

After a few days, when Mom asked me how my summer was going, I answered "couldn't be better" in my most cheerful tone.

This is what "fine" sounds like, I thought.

"Fine" didn't last long, though. About a week into my new routine, something shifted, and the drifting didn't seem to work anymore. I woke up one morning, early, and couldn't go back to sleep. And lying there in my bed, the sheets all tangled and bunched and sweaty, I found I was totally, absolutely, incredibly bored.

So I got up and wandered around the house, but that didn't help. I was still bored. Bored with myself. Bored with the house, and my books, and dumb YouTube. A few times that day, I found my phone full of texts, group messages from people I never talked to anymore but who hadn't thought to leave me off. They were boring too, mostly just different versions of *Hey!* and *How's your summer going?* I never replied, but I still scrolled through them, to see what people were up to. And—I couldn't help it—to see what Tess was doing.

Ever since we were really little kids, Tess and I had done everything together. Preschool. Girl Scouts. Dance class. We'd shared a fort in my backyard, and licked each others' lollipops, as gross as that seemed now. And every Saturday night, up until last year, we'd had a sleepover. We took turns telling each other bedtime stories, and slept tip to toe, with a pillow at each end of the bed, so I'd wake up in the morning staring at Tess's feet, and that seemed normal. I'd kept pajamas at her house and a toothbrush.

I wondered if my toothbrush was still there, its frayed plastic bristles collecting dust. Or if they'd tossed it by now.

And here I hadn't talked to her in a week. So I couldn't help it. When a text came in, and I heard that little *ping!*, I'd sort of wake up a little more than usual. Just for a second. It was funny how that worked, with phones. Wherever I was, whatever I was doing, when I got a text, it made me sit up straight, made my heart race just a little. *Someone is thinking of me*, I'd think.

Even if my very next thought was *But it doesn't really matter.*

Anyway, sitting around the house watching TV and waiting for texts I didn't care about very much wore out, and finally I couldn't take it anymore.

So on Thursday, I put on actual pants that weren't leggings and walked through my front door. Into the blazing, burning Georgia sun I hadn't seen in a week. So bright it made me squint.

The problem was that even in my actual pants, I really had no place to go and nobody to go there with. Everyone else was *somewhere*. It was June seventh. The people who went to interesting and exotic places were off being interesting and exotic. The people who went to camp were already at camp. I'd always been a camp person, and so I had no clue—what did people do in the summer, all summer, at home? With no camp counselors and schedules? Arts and crafts? Ropes courses? Free swim? Summer was a long time when no one was planning it for you.

I walked to the end of my street and then turned right onto Woodland, and that felt pretty okay, walking, after a week in the house. Stretching. Seeing stuff. There were flowers to stare at in people's yards. In front of the yellow house on the corner, James the brat was screaming his face off, and his mom, Kate, was looking like she wanted to scream *her* face off, and that was sort of interesting for a minute. Anyway, it was loud.

I waved at them, and Kate waved back, so then I thought

about stopping over to say hi, but James was still fussing, and I didn't really know them very well anyway. They'd only been in the neighborhood for a few years. I kept going.

The feral cats that lived in the church parking lot were sleeping in a patch of sun by the dumpster, and I stopped to say hi to them. They wouldn't let you touch them, but they didn't mind visitors, and I liked to watch them roll in the dust and lick themselves. At the corner, someone had scrawled new graffiti on the back of the stop sign. "GO TO HELL," it said, "OR GO TO MARIETTA." Funny.

After a few minutes, I realized I was walking faster, and I wasn't sure why. I felt like I *wanted* something, like I was walking *toward* something, but I wasn't sure what that might be. For a few blocks, I tried to see who had the best political yard sign. "Injustice Anywhere Is a Threat to Justice Everywhere" was in first place, but then on one street, every single house had a "Black Lives Matter" sign, so that block won.

Finally, I got sweaty enough to turn home, but when I strolled back down Woodland, Miss Sandy glanced up from her flower bed and gave me a suspicious look, kind of following me with her eyes. I couldn't figure out what that meant at first, and then it occurred to me that maybe she didn't recognize me. Was I tall enough now to be mistaken for an up-to-no-good teenager? Was that possible? I waved at Miss Sandy, but she didn't wave back, just turned her white head down to stare at her irises as she weeded.

My mom often complained about the up-to-no-good teenagers in the neighborhood, who always seemed to be skating or wandering around at dusk. And I thought that was funny, because as normal as my mom was now, if you looked at pictures of her from college, you could see that she and her friends had been totally up-to-no-good teenagers themselves. All the boys in those pictures had long hair and tattoos, and all the girls had piercings and colorful streaks in their hair. But whenever I'd accused her of being a troublemaker herself, Mom claimed *that's* how she knew what sort of trouble teenagers got into.

What I needed was a dog. Nobody looked at you funny if you walked around aimlessly with a dog on a leash. Maybe I'd start a dog-walking business. Dad would love that. And then I'd have something to write about in August, if any of my teachers demanded to know *What I Did over Summer Vacation.* That would be handy, since *I wore a lot of pajamas and occasionally wandered aimlessly in actual pants* probably wasn't going to cut it.

Maybe it was because of Miss Sandy's suspicious look that I decided to take the long way home that day. Maybe I did it because I was thinking wandering thoughts, and so my feet were feeling wandery. Maybe because some crazy sort of magic led me there. But whatever the reason, I turned left off Woodland onto Mercer and headed for Red's Farm.

Mercer was a funny street, more of an alley than a road.

Or maybe a country lane. Unpaved and surrounded by trees and brush. It didn't look like it belonged in the city any more than the farm did. This was a secret place, an odd overgrown pocket, a quiet spot buried in the busy middle of Atlanta. I always slowed down on Mercer. I couldn't help kicking at the gravel, stopping for honeysuckle or the wild raspberries that sometimes crept up on the chain-link fence. Where the road dead-ended at a wooden gate, I stopped, lifted the latch, and stepped inside.

I hadn't been to Red's Farm in forever. It was private property, but Farmer Red, the guy who'd owned the place for as long as I could remember, didn't mind if you hung out, just so long as you didn't mess with the chickens or leave any trash behind. It was funny to be there now, alone. Everything was silent and green. Usually someone was wandering around in the distance, along the back field or down by the community garden, but today the place was dead silent. I stood at the top of the hill and looked around. At the rope swing hanging limp; at the rusty old pump, dripping; at a single yellow butterfly coasting on the still, hot afternoon air.

But then, suddenly, there was a burst of cool wind, so unexpected it made me jump. It was like the air at the mouth of a cave. It only lasted a second, just one big gasp, like the whole farm was breathing around me. It came and went, clear and bright. I closed my eyes, and when I opened them, I felt . . . refreshed. I started walking down the hill.

It wasn't possible to be there without remembering. Summer-evening walks with my family down the gravel road, and picnics on a heavy blanket laid in the tall grass. We'd take turns on the rope swing, and then run back to the blanket for cold Publix fried chicken and strawberries, warm from the sun. Mom and Dad would sip their beers and we'd wait for the fireflies to come out. That wasn't something we'd done in a long time. Years. Maybe picnics stopped when kids quit catching fireflies? Or maybe my parents had just gotten busy and forgotten about picnics?

I pushed the thought from my head as I headed down the hill toward the creek. I was only going to walk along the creek bed home, trudge through sand and kudzu. *That* was why I was here. It was just a way home. That was all I ever meant to do—go home that day.

It's funny to think now about how everything might have turned out, or *not* turned out, if I hadn't cut through Red's Farm. It would have been a different June, that's for sure. It would have been a different summer, and a different everything. But I *did* walk into Red's Farm, and I *did* stop at the creek, and when I stopped, I saw her for the first time.

Jasper.

She was sprawled out on a big, flat rock in the middle of the creek. The same rock where we used to play pirates when we were little, in our red bandannas and eye patches. She was still and her eyes were closed and her hair was like a cloud of red fuzz all around her face—so frizzy and curly that when she was lying back like that, her profile kind of disappeared into her pouf of hair. That was the first thing I remember thinking, that her hair was totally huge. But in a wonderful way. Like she was some beautiful clown.

She looked like she was sleeping, but I couldn't tell, so I stood there; and after a few minutes—probably too long for me to be watching a stranger sleeping on a rock—she swatted at something near her face, likely a mosquito, and sat up.

"Oh hey, stranger!" she said when she saw me.

Just that.

Hey, stranger.

Is it weird if I say that I knew then, at that very moment? I knew that something was happening, something important, and different . . . like in a fairy tale? That nothing would be the same ever again? It *is* weird. It seems impossible. But that was how it felt. Like something from one of my books. Or that's how I remember it feeling, anyway. Like the temperature suddenly shifted, and I couldn't say whether it was a few degrees cooler or warmer, only that my skin could sense the change.

I think I waved. I think I called back, "Hey!" I think I was probably a little too loud. It's hard to remember exactly. But then I walked over. Right up to her rock. Which had always been *our* rock, for years and years, as long as I could remember.

"I thought I was all alone," she said, laughing. "I must

look crazy, lying here on a rock in the middle of the creek, like I'm a mermaid or something. It was just so nice out. And feel this . . ." She patted the stone beside her. "It's warm from the sun."

I smiled back and shook my head. "Not crazy at all! I know. Me and my . . . I do that here too. All the time."

That wasn't actually true. But it *had* been true. Once . . .

After that I wasn't sure what to say. Finally I came up with "Are you . . . new? In Ormewood Park?"

She nodded. "Yeah, pretty new."

"So, where did you live before this?" I asked after another few seconds of silence. "Before you moved?"

"Not far away," she said. "North. Near Kennesaw."

"Oh," I said. "Cool." Even though it wasn't especially.

"Yeah."

She kept looking at me silently. And even though it didn't seem like she was expecting anything, I tried again. "I've lived here since I was a baby. On Loring Street, near the end of Woodland. Over that way." I pointed vaguely in the direction of home.

"Nice," she said, glancing back over her shoulder and peering into the trees. As though she had mutant superpowers and could see my house, a half mile away. "It's pretty, this neighborhood. The houses are so cute, and I like all the big front porches. It feels almost like the country here, even though we're still in Atlanta."

"Yeah," I said. "The houses are . . . old."

For a magical life-changing moment, there was nothing magical or life-changing about this conversation.

It was her turn to say something, but she didn't. I thought she probably wanted me to go away and was giving me a polite signal. But at the same time, she was smiling in that odd, calm, encouraging way.

When I couldn't stand the silence any longer, I glanced all around me—up at the canopy of thick trees, then back up the hill behind me, and finally down the creek, past the new girl on the rock, into the jungle of kudzu I'd need to push through to get home. I felt strangely locked in that moment, as if under some sort of spell, a power stronger than my own two feet.

At last I said, "Well, I guess I'll go now."

"Okay," she said pleasantly enough.

"Okay," I repeated.

"Have a nice day," she said, waving. Which people said all the time, and probably didn't really mean, but I swear, in that moment, she sounded like she really meant it. Like she genuinely hoped I'd have an especially nice day.

"You too!" I replied as I began to move at last, skirting around the rock and trudging a few feet down the creek bed, away. Feeling . . .

What? Disappointed. But more than that. And for some reason, I just couldn't walk away without even knowing her name. I turned back, to find her staring after me, no longer smiling. She had a different look on her face now. Watchful—her eyes were big and solemn. But she also seemed a little . . . lost. Like she wanted to ask me something too.

"Hey," I said. "I'm . . . Leah. Leah Davidson. In case we ever see each other again. Here, maybe. Or around, since you're in the neighborhood now, or . . . whatever. Just so you know. I'm Leah."

She nodded slowly, as if she understood something I wasn't sure I'd said. She looked strangely serious when she replied, "Okay, Leah. And I'm Jasper."

That was all.

I turned and kept walking down the creek bed, forcing myself to keep moving forward, toward the wild green tangle. Staring at my sandals as they sank into the damp pebbly mix of dirt and sand. Trying to avoid stepping on the broken bits of bottle and old rusty cans from the storm drains that fed the creek. Brushing the scratchy kudzu out of the way as I went. Just moving forward, home. My feet got wet.

"Jasper," I whispered into the kudzu and the mosquitos. "Jasper."

And that was when I realized—I was very, very lonely.

TOTALLY IN CONTROL

I went back to the farm every day after that. Partly because I had nothing else to do . . . but mostly hoping to see Jasper again.

She was never there.

Each time I went, I took a book along and a snack. So that it would look like I just happened to be having a lazy, old-fashioned summer day, roaming the neighborhood, reading, a happy loner. Each time, I sat somewhere different. One day I sat at the splintery picnic table under the big oak tree. Another day I climbed up into the rusty old tractor my mom had never let me sit on when I was littler, as if she was afraid it might suddenly start up and carry me away.

But it didn't make a bit of difference where I sat. I'd open my book and sit with it in front of me, scanning the pages, pretending to read, but I couldn't seem to fall into the story, ever. It was like my eyes were reading the words, but my mind was listening for footsteps. So I'd end up scrolling around in my phone instead, but not paying much attention to that either.

Each day I made sure to stop by Jasper's rock and wait a few minutes. It almost felt like I'd imagined her there, conjured her up. It seemed likelier that she had gone on vacation with her family to Tybee Island, or maybe down to Florida. That was what people did in June.

Then one Sunday night, I got a text from Liv, a few streets over. We hadn't hung out outside of school in forever. Not since our moms carpooled together when we were in third grade. But now she was telling me that she was going to join the middle school cross-country team, and she had to train over the summer, and she didn't want to do it by herself, and did I want meet up with her tomorrow morning at the coffee shop and then go for a run before it got too hot?

I was not someone who ever really wanted to run, anywhere. I was so bad at sports my kindergarten teacher had once called home to talk to my parents about how I needed to *work on my jumping.* Dad used to love telling that story when my parents had their friends over. "Leah, how's the jumping coming?" He'd chuckle with his friends. "We're going to get her a jumping tutor."

But I was bored and desperate enough that it almost seemed like it might be fun to get a muffin and hang out at Joe's, even if it meant jogging afterward. So I found myself sleepy but awake at six thirty, tying my laces and pulling my hair into a tangled ponytail.

My parents were surprised to see me up.

"Oh. Are you going out somewhere?" Mom asked vaguely.

Dad looked me up and down, took note of my running shoes, and gave a quick nod of approval. "Need any cash?" he wanted to know. "You should never be anywhere without cab fare, remember. House rule."

"I know, Dad." I said. "But I have a bunch of birthday money left. I'm fine." He didn't seem to register that, and he pulled a twenty out of his wallet, sort of shoved it in my direction. So I took the cash and bent over to slide it down inside my sock.

"Sit down," said Mom. "Let me make you breakfast. Pancakes?"

"Pancakes?" I said, looking up at her. "Really?"

"What's wrong with pancakes?" Dad looked annoyed, but I wasn't sure what I'd done, exactly.

"Nothing . . . I just . . ."

I couldn't remember the last time my mom had made pancakes, even though they used to be a Sunday-morning ritual. With blueberries or chocolate chips. The house smelling a little smoky from the griddle, but in a nice way. I looked at my mom's face and wondered what would happen if I said yes. If I just nodded. Would we really all sit down and eat pancakes together? Would the house smell warm and happy, like browned butter and crumbs? Would Dad pour way too much syrup on his, and laugh when Mom rolled her eyes?

Mom was still waiting.

I shook my head. "No, I'm good," I said as I sort of edged past my dad, dug a water bottle out of the cabinet, and filled it at the sink. Then I waved goodbye and headed outside. The kitchen screen door slammed behind me.

The truth was that I was early to meet Liv, but pancakes or no pancakes, I really didn't want to sit at the table and watch them chew and sip right now. Mom periodically trying to start a conversation. Dad staring at his phone. Dinner each night was plenty of that.

I think I walked along the creek that morning out of habit. Because I'd been doing it on my afternoon scouting missions, hunting for Jasper. I don't really think I had her on my mind at that moment. I was thinking about pancakes, and trying not to think about pancakes. I was chugging my water and stretching my legs.

But then I came around the bend, near the pile of old tires, and stepped out of the kudzu jungle, to find Jasper's back to me, bent over something. When I saw her, I gasped, then choked a mouthful of water and spit it out, coughing.

She whirled around. "Crap!" she shouted. But then, in a quieter voice, she added, "Oh, hey, Leah. You scared me."

I stood there, water dripping all down my shirt, still sputtering. I wiped my mouth with the back of my hand. "Sorry," I said.

Then I noticed. Jasper was wearing a nightgown.

No matter how I tried, I couldn't not stare at her. She was so out of place, with her big hair, long bare legs, and the nightgown—a billowing pink T-shirt that read Zzzzzzzzzzz . . . There was a sleepy-eyed teddy bear on it. The teddy bear was purple.

It had to be the ugliest nightgown in the history of nightgowns.

Jasper caught me staring and glanced down. "I'm . . . uh . . ."

It was like she was a different person from our first meeting. All of her calm was gone. Her brown eyes were huge in her face. They looked almost frightened.

"Are you okay?" I asked. "Why are you . . . well, what are you doing?" I think we both knew I really meant *Why on earth are you up at Red's Farm at the crack of dawn in your nightie?*

But then, in that moment, a funny thing happened. It was like I watched Jasper decide how to *feel*. Like I could actually see it happen, the transformation. One minute she was freaked out and embarrassed and unsure. And then, in a split second, she wasn't anymore. Her mouth closed, her eyes softened, and her shoulders shifted back. She flashed me the same big smile that she had a week before and answered me with a shrug.

Then I noticed the big pile of crumpled laundry on the rock behind her. She saw me notice it too. And the small bottle of dish soap beside it. It took me a minute to put the pieces together. "Wait. Are you washing your clothes?" I asked. "In the *creek*?"

"Well, if I had anything else clean to wear, do you think I'd be wearing *this* in public?" Jasper said with a grimace, holding out the hem of her shirt and doing a little curtsy. "There's something wrong with the water at our house, and the people from the city haven't come to fix it. But all my stuff is dirty, and Mom is at work, so she wasn't able to take me to the laundromat. I couldn't stand wearing my gross dirty jeans anymore, but I remembered this place and came back. It was this or taking the bus to the laundromat in this nightshirt, my bare legs touching the seats."

And I guessed that made sense, even if it was a little bizarre. It explained the nightgown, anyway.

"Okay," I said. "Sure." Then I glanced from the pile of clothes back to Jasper. "You know, if you want to, you can just come use the washer and dryer at my house. If you don't mind walking a few more blocks in your pj's."

Something flashed over her face, and then she smiled. "Really?"

"Sure," I said. "Why not?"

"But what will your parents say when I walk in like this?"

"They're leaving for work soon. And even if they're still there, they won't notice. They don't notice much."

"Seriously?"

"Well, maybe my mom would notice, but she'd be all nervous and extra friendly and tell you she liked your shirt. Even if she didn't."

Jasper looked down at the shirt and back up at me, "Be real," she said. "*Nobody* could like this thing."

I couldn't help laughing at that. "Yeah, it's pretty awful."

"Hey . . . if you really mean it," said Jasper, "I'd be super grateful."

"Sure," I said, feeling a rush, a thrill. I guess I hadn't actually expected her to say yes. This was the most interesting thing that had happened all summer. All year. Maybe even longer than that. "Do you want me to help carry anything?"

"Oh, no, I can get it," she said. She turned around and started scooping up her wet things, shoving all the clothes—wet and dry both—into a big red sweatshirt. Then she scooped the big laundry ball up in both arms. "But thanks!"

As I led the way home, down the creek bed, and held

the kudzu back for Jasper and her armload of clothes, I had a thought. "Hey, Jasper—why didn't you bring a laundry basket?"

She laughed into the pile of clothes. "Because I'm an idiot sometimes, that's why!"

I laughed too. "Well, sure. Everyone is."

EXTRA REAL

It usually takes me a little while to talk when I meet someone new, but for some reason, the whole way home, I talked and talked and talked. I thought maybe I was being annoying, but I couldn't seem to stop myself from giving Jasper a guided tour of the neighborhood. It was like I needed her to love it, and so I found myself pointing out things I hadn't thought about in a long time. All the things I'd been walking past without noticing them. And once I started talking, the words just didn't stop.

As we walked along, I pointed out the protected overhang beside the creek where homeless guys sit when it rains. "They sing sometimes," I said. "You can hear them up at the farm."

We turned onto Berne Street, and I pointed out the yard with all the bottle trees in it, blue glass bottles stuck on every bare branch. A few houses past that, we came to the cracked stretch of sidewalk with the hollow tree growing up through it. Some mysterious neighbor had made the tree into a geocache years ago, and occasionally they still hid a tin box of hard candies there too. But when we looked inside, the box was empty.

"Oh well," said Jasper. "Next time."

Then, before I knew it, we were standing in front of Tess's house. I hadn't meant to stop walking, but somehow, that's what happened. I felt my thighs graze the hedge of gardenias that separated the familiar green house from the sidewalk, and glanced down at the sweet white blossoms. I reached out a hand to touch one. So soft. How many times had I picked them, to wear in my hair or make a bouquet for Mom?

"Who lives here?" asked Jasper as though she could tell it wasn't just any house.

"Oh, this is . . . Tess's house," I said. "But she's not home."

"Who's Tess? A friend?"

I nodded. Because it was true of course, even now. But there was so much I wasn't sure how to say. I didn't say that Tess's mother had given me my first tampon, when I got my period while making hand-cranked peach ice cream in their yard. I didn't say that her mom was my mom's best friend from high school. Or that I hadn't set foot in her house for months now, and there was no way I could really explain that fact.

I only looked from the green house to Jasper and nodded. "Yeah, she's a friend. But I think she's on vacation right now." My voice sounded funny coming out when I said that, sort of hoarse and quiet, so I cleared my throat. Then I turned to the house next door, and pointed. "But now, *that* house is pretty funny. The guys who live there—Ed and Johnny—they have a yard sale every Saturday, full of things like half-burned candles and old remote controls. There's a bowl of batteries, but no way to know whether they're dead or not. So much junk."

If Jasper could tell that I was changing the subject, she didn't say anything about it. She just said, "Every single week?"

"Yep!" I said. "I don't even know where it all comes from? Maybe the house is just getting emptier and emptier, week by week. One day there won't be anything left inside it, and then they'll move away."

"Weird," said Jasper.

We started walking again, and I pointed out the dead-end alley where the basketball hoop was. But as we passed a big new house going up, its raw wood gleaming yellow in the sunlight, it was Jasper's turn to point. "Whoa! Now, that's a mansion, huh? Who has that much money? Can you even imagine living in a house like that?"

"It *is* pretty huge," I said. "Hey, what if you were at one end of the house, and you had to pee, and the bathroom was at the other end? You might not make it, the place is so big."

Jasper laughed. "It probably doesn't matter. It probably has, like, seventeen bathrooms."

"Good point," I said. "Still, I bet it echoes."

"Yeah."

"Anyway, there's a bunch of those being built now around here. My parents used to talk about it all the time, when rich people started moving into the neighborhood. It's funny. They have these big lawns that none of them mow themselves."

By that point, we were nearing my street, so I pointed out the fig tree in the middle of the roundabout. "We helped plant it," I said. "When I was little."

"Oh, figs," said Jasper. "Are they ripe?"

I shook my head. "Not until July. I don't think. Can't remember for sure. One year we picked them and tried to make jam, but it was actually pretty gross. That's the kind of thing my mom used to pretend to do—stuff like making jam or quilting. She's awful at it all, and she doesn't usually finish. Just buys whatever equipment she needs, and then it ends up in the garage. Does your mom do stuff like that? Crafty stuff?" I looked back at Jasper, but she had a vacant look on her face— like she was staring through me.

"No," she said. "Not at all."

"Oh," I said. "Well, then what's she like?"

"Who?" asked Jasper.

"Your mom."

Jasper shook her head. "Not crafty," she said. She turned

away, to reach up and touch a green fig. "This sure is a fruity neighborhood. There's all kinds of stuff growing at the farm too. Strawberries and whatnot."

"Yeah, but we aren't supposed to pick any of that," I said, scratching the back of my head. "Unless Farmer Red's there and he offers. Like, if he has too many cucumbers or something, sometimes he'll send me home with a few. But mostly he saves what he grows, I think maybe to sell at farmers markets around town."

"I guess that makes sense," said Jasper.

"Yeah."

By that point we reached my house, so I turned and pointed. "This is me," I said, starting up the driveway. Our house was brick with white trim and a big low front porch, like most of the houses in the neighborhood. The bushes in front were overgrown, and the grass was high and messy. I hadn't noticed how bad it was until this very minute.

I opened the gate, and Jasper followed me into the backyard and through the side door into the kitchen.

"Oh! The air-conditioning feels so good in here," she said when she stepped into the room. "It's like walking into a refrigerator."

"Yeah, my dad keeps it really cold," I said. "He and Mom argue about it. She says it's better for the environment to turn it off, and *he* says it's better for their marriage to keep it going full blast."

"Well, I feel a little bad for the environment," said Jasper. "But I'm not complaining. It's delicious in here."

"Delicious," I echoed. "Yeah, I guess it is."

Somehow, the strangeness of the whole morning hit me then, and I found myself staring at Jasper, at this girl I barely knew. She gripped her dripping bundle, in her pink teddy bear T-shirt and her flip-flops, in the middle of our kitchen, which still smelled like coffee and toast. The ghosts of breakfast.

"Okay, so, laundry," I said, leading her straight through the kitchen and into the room we called "the office" because there happened to be a desk there. For months, the desk had been stacked with unopened tubes of Hanukkah wrapping paper that Mom had bought on clearance somewhere. But of course it wasn't Hanukkah, so they just sat there on the desk, covered in shiny blue dreidels, collecting dust. "The washer and dryer are over here, in this closet. And here's the detergent, and dryer sheets, and a basket. Sorry if it's all a little messy right now."

"You think *this* is messy?" Jasper set down her bundle and glanced around the room. "You should see where I live. This place is amazing."

"Really?" I looked from the cluttered desk to the overfull bookshelf and tried to see it that way.

I'd always liked our house fine, but it wasn't the kind of house people usually complimented. Certainly not *amazing*. It was regular, a *house* house. It was true that we had a nice big back deck. And there was lots of strange art on the walls that my dad had made, or friends of his, back when he was young and trying to be an artist. I tried to see all of that now the way Jasper was seeing it. But the couch had cat claw marks Mom always covered with a blanket when people came over, and there were crayon scribbles on the wall from a long time ago that couldn't be cleaned completely.

Back when she used to joke more, Mom would say that she preferred a *relaxed* lifestyle, that she didn't ever want to feel like her house was too nice to put her feet up on the coffee table. That was funny to me, because feet or no feet, Mom was never really *relaxed*. She was always dashing somewhere in a hurry, and she usually had a list of fourteen things in her pocket that she needed to do that day and tell you about the minute you saw her. Mom *stressed*. But she was also kind of sloppy. I think *relaxed* just made her feel better about herself than *sloppy*.

"I think it's beautiful," said Jasper as she unpacked the sweatshirt and started tossing everything in the washer. "I like how every room is a different color. And the furniture is so old and wooden. Like in an antique store." She pointed to a stack of old peach crates Dad had fastened together for shelving. "I love this."

"Well, thanks, but this is nothing compared to some of my friends' houses. They have pools, a few of them. There are some really rich kids at my school. You know, living in those mansions we saw."

"Well, nobody *I* know has a pool," said Jasper. She grinned and added, "Feel free to introduce me to your friends!"

"I guess they're more just kids I know, not really friends," I said honestly. Over the years, I'd gotten invited to a lot of birthday parties because of Tess. She just kind of knew everybody, and somehow she always sat at the center of the lunch table. I'd felt lucky to be her best friend. Popular by association.

"Anyway, you should see my place. This house is nice for sure." Jasper slammed the door of the washer and turned it on. Then she spun around to look at me again, and I wasn't sure what came next. The laundry would be in the washer for forty-two minutes, according to the green blinking digital numbers. And then the dryer. We had an hour or two, at least.

"Hey, while we're waiting, do you want something to eat?" I asked. "I haven't had breakfast yet."

"Why not?" said Jasper. "I can always eat."

And, wow, could she ever. I got out bagels and cereal and fruit and juice and yogurt and granola, thinking that Jasper could pick what she liked. It turned out she liked everything. Lots of everything.

Sitting at the kitchen table, we didn't talk for a bit. Just chewed and sipped. But then I was licking some cream cheese off my finger when Jasper suddenly stood up, walked over to a cabinet, opened it, and plucked out a coffee mug, as if she'd known right where it was. Just like that. Like magic.

"Wow, how did you know where to find that?" I asked.

Jasper shrugged. "Everyone keeps coffee mugs above the coffee maker, silly," she said. "Haven't you ever noticed?"

"I guess not," I said.

Watching Jasper pour herself a cup of leftover coffee from the pot, I felt a funny happy twinge. It was nice to see someone so at home in my house. Tess had always helped herself to food whenever she was over, but that was different. She'd grown up here.

After Jasper had stirred in plenty of sugar and a dribble of milk, she rejoined me at the table, where she leaned back in her chair with both hands around the mug. She took a sip of coffee and grinned at me happily over the rim. *Just like my mother*, I thought. *Only the exact opposite.* Jasper was relaxed for sure.

"Leah?" she said.

"Yes?" I was nervous for some reason. Something in her even stare and her tone.

But then all she said was "Thank you. Very, very, very, very much."

That caught me by surprise. "Oh! Sure! Anytime. No big deal."

Jasper shook her head, like I hadn't understood her. "No," she said. "It *is* a big deal, for me. So for real, thank you. This is so much nicer than any morning I've had in a while. Just great."

Just great. There was something funny in her voice when

she said that. Something different, almost sad. "Is everything okay?" I asked.

Jasper nodded right away. "Oh, sure. I'm fine. Just . . . I'm new, you know? And I haven't really met people. I guess . . . I've been keeping to myself. I didn't even know I was looking for a friend."

At the word *friend*, I could feel my cheeks pinking up, hot. "Oh, whatever, no worries," I said, glancing away. Then I stood, pushed out my chair, and headed for the bathroom. "Back in a sec," I called over my shoulder as casually as I could.

In the bathroom, I turned on the faucet, stood over the sink, and watched the water drain down. Why did I feel so weird all of a sudden? Something about Jasper made me nervous. Everything just felt *so much*. Everything felt like . . . it mattered.

The thing is, Jasper was exactly right. It was the nicest morning I could remember in a long time. It was easy. We were friends. We *were* friends. Just like that. Talking about nothing much over breakfast, or walking home in the sunshine. It had been a long time since anything had felt so good to me.

I could feel it like weather. The way you sometimes know it will rain before you see a single cloud. I could feel the change of it, just like I had felt it at Red's Farm the moment I saw her. What kind of girl sprawls on a rock in the sun, alone, and doesn't feel embarrassed when you catch her? What kind of girl does her laundry in the creek? What kind of girl follows a stranger home, and then eats the last bagel, with a smile? She was like something from a book. Like I'd wished her into existence, though of course I knew that wasn't possible.

I splashed water on my face and took a deep breath. Then I patted my face dry on a stiff towel and flushed the toilet.

When I got back to the table, Jasper was sipping her coffee and leafing through a *National Geographic*, which we got in the mail each month but nobody ever actually read. They just stacked up by the fireplace in a basket. Jasper pretended I hadn't just gotten all weird and blushy a few minutes before, and she glanced up at me in a totally normal way as I sat down.

"Hey, so, anyway . . . ," she said. "Where were you going this morning, when you turned up at the farm?"

"What?" I said. Then I froze. "Oh, *no*."

"What?"

"Liv," I said, reaching for the phone in my pocket. "I totally forget about Liv."

I looked down, and, sure enough, I had four messages.

Where RU?
UR LATE.
I'm leaving now.
Thanks a lot.

I sighed, texted *Sorry*, and set my phone down on the table. "Ugh," I said. "I was on my way to meet someone. I said I'd run with her. This girl I know."

"Oof," said Jasper, closing her magazine and looking up at me. "Sorry if I screwed it up with my crazy laundry situation."

"Eh, it's okay," I said, sliding back down into my chair. "It's not like it's the end of the world. I'd way rather be doing this. And Liv will be fine."

"Yeah," said Jasper. "Not like someone died, or something."

"Umm, yeah," I said. "Nothing like that."

Then there was a funny pause, and Jasper said, "Are you sure it's okay? Do you need to go and meet up with her? Because if you're just being polite about this, we can go and I can come back later for my stuff."

I shook my head quickly. "No, no, no . . . seriously. It's no big deal. Sorry if I seem weird. I'm fine."

"Everyone's late sometimes," said Jasper. "I'm sure your friend will forgive you."

"Sure," I said. "I guess. But the truth is, it doesn't matter much. Liv isn't a very good friend."

"What do you mean?" asked Jasper.

"Just . . . ," I said, reaching for a banana and peeling it slowly. "You know how sometimes you have backup friends? People you hang out with when your real friends are gone?"

Jasper nodded. "I *think* so."

I broke the banana and offered half to Jasper. She took it. "Well, Liv is one of those. I've known her a long time, and she lives nearby, but I don't really like her very much. I mean, I don't dislike her. She's fine. There's nothing *wrong* with her. She's just not my *real* friend. And I'm not hers either. She called me because she didn't have anyone else to hang out with, I'm sure. She's like . . . an acquaintance. Someone to fill in the gaps."

I took a bite of banana and thought about what I'd said.

Jasper chewed her banana too. "Ah, yeah. I know what you mean. I know exactly. In fact, I have a lot of gaps myself right now."

"Really?" I asked. It was the first real thing Jasper had said about her own life since we'd met.

"You have no idea," said Jasper.

That was true. I didn't have any idea. But I wasn't sure what to say in reply, so I just said, "So . . ."

Jasper looked at me funny, squinted one eye, like she was measuring something. "Honestly," she said, "it's been a while since I had much of anything else. Sometimes it feels like my life is *all* gaps." Then she stopped squinting, and her eyes were clear and sharp on me. Intense. "Does that sound strange?"

Right away I shook my head, hard. "No," I said. "Not at all. It sounds . . . familiar."

And that was the truth. Though I hadn't realized how true it was until the words were out of my mouth.

"But then," said Jasper, holding my gaze. "Then there are also people who fill the gaps when you really need them to. The big gaps. When it matters. Once in a while, I meet someone like that. And I can just tell we'll be friends. Real friends. You know what I mean?"

For one long moment we were staring at each other, and she was right, of course, and we both knew it. Then the sun shifted outside the window, and the kitchen was full of light, bouncing golden off the walls.

I blinked. I almost wanted to cry. But I wasn't sad at all. My eyes were aching in a happy way. My bones felt looser. It was like a spell had broken, and the whole house felt brighter, better. So I nodded.

"Yes," I said.

Suddenly Jasper jumped up from the table and grinned, big and goofy. "Hey, Leah, while we wait for the laundry, can we maybe . . . watch a movie? Would that be okay with you?"

"Are you serious? Of course!" I said, and grinned back at her. Just as big. Like I was a mirror. It felt so good to grin like that. To mean it. "That would be great," I said, and I stood up too, started for the living room. Jasper followed.

Of *course* we could. We could watch a movie, like normal people do, like friends do. We could sit on the old gray couch, in a pile of pillows and blankets. We could paint our nails if we wanted. We could sip fizzy water and stop the movie periodically to joke around. We could watch *two* movies, if we felt like

46

it. We could make nachos later. Or ramen.

Because that was what you did, when you didn't go to camp in the summer. You had a friend over. That was a regular thing to do, if you were thirteen and you had the house to yourself and it was summer vacation and your parents weren't going to be home for hours. You had *fun*. I'd forgotten, but now, suddenly, I remembered.

Jasper had reminded me how to *be*.

SEALED UP TIGHT

In the living room, Jasper flopped onto the couch and leaned back into the unmatched throw pillows to stretch. When she did, I noticed that her legs were scratched and covered with mosquito bites. Like little-kid legs. Elementary school legs.

Jasper caught me looking. "Ugh," she said. "This shirt is so stupid." She pulled her knees up inside it, to cover them. "It used to be my sister's, a long time ago. I'm not even sure why I still wear it. Have you ever seen anything so awful?"

"Actually . . . yes," I said. "In fact I have. Wait here a minute." I ran from the room.

"Leah! Where are you going?" Jasper called after me into the hallway. But I didn't answer.

When I reentered the room a minute later, I couldn't help singing out, "Ta-DA." I was rewarded with a big laugh from Jasper at the sight of my pajamas. My footie pajamas. My one-piece bright yellow footie pajamas. With orange cuffs. They were getting too small, but I could still wiggle into them.

"Yow!" Jasper shouted. "You look . . . amazing!"

"Don't I just?" I turned in a slow circle. "They were a Hanukkah present from my grandma when I was a kid. I think they make me look like a duck. A big, insane duck." I stuck my thumbs into my armpits and flapped my wings.

Jasper burst out laughing again. "Yes, you do. You look exactly like a duck." She pulled the old red blanket off the back of the couch and draped it over her legs. "Much appreciated. I feel less alone in my idiocy now."

"You're very welcome," I said, settling in beside her on the couch and clicking the TV on. "Happy to be an idiot whenever you need one. So, what are you in the mood for?"

"Oh, whatever . . . ," said Jasper.

"No!" I insisted. "You're the guest. *You* pick. Do you have a favorite movie?"

"Well, if you really want to know," Jasper said, "I *do*, actually. I'm pretty much always in the mood for . . . *Harry Potter*."

"No way!" I shouted. "Me too. Even though I've seen them all about seventeen times."

"Really?" asked Jasper.

I nodded. "Totally. Best movies ever. Books too."

"I don't know why," Jasper said with a sigh. "But no matter how old I get, nothing else ever seems quite as good. Even if the effects are kind of dumb."

"It's the magic for me," I said. "The idea that all the impossible things might be possible, right *there*, at the other end of my chimney." I looked at the cold fireplace that nobody had used in a year. "That the world isn't only . . . *this*."

"Exactly!" said Jasper. "For years, I seriously hoped I'd get a letter when I turned eleven. And then I'd leave for Hogwarts. You know? Run away from everything . . ."

I nodded. "I do. I really do."

"I just feel like everything would make more sense if we all had spells and wands and we could fix things with magic, and there was another world, where things were different than they actually are in this world."

"Right?" I said, surfing around until I found the first movie, and clicked to rent. Then I held the remote out like a wand and waved it in the air dramatically. *"Accio Harry Potter and the Sorcerer's Stone!"*

The movie started, and for a little while, we were quiet, just watching and occasionally mouthing the words to the movie together, and laughing. Until the washer dinged, and Jasper got up to move her stuff to the dryer. I paused the movie.

After a minute, she came back with a big fat square of lint

draped over her head. "What's the deal? Does nobody change the lint trap in this house?"

"Oh," I said. "Yeah, like I said, my mom forgets stuff sometimes."

"Fair enough," said Jasper. "But you should keep this one. I think maybe you broke a world record for lint. *Look* at it! It's truly amazing." She held it out to me.

"Ha," I said, rubbing the thick square of felt. "It *is* pretty ridiculous. But if I said anything to my mom, her eyes would get all sad and her forehead would crease, and she'd run her hand through her hair. Then she'd murmur something about trying to do better, and add *lint trap* to a list somewhere and then lose it. In her purse. And I'd feel guilty. All because of this tiny little thing I said. It isn't worth it."

"Isn't that a Jewish thing, guilt? I've read about that."

"I didn't think guilt was *only* Jewish. But how'd you know we were Jewish?"

"You just mentioned Hanukkah, you goof," she said, punching me lightly on the arm. "But also that doohickey on your door. What's it called?"

"Oh, the mezuzah, yeah."

"Yes, the meh-zu-zah," she said, repeating it carefully after me.

"Anyway, I guess it's not *just* Mom's job to do laundry. I could help too, with the dumb lint trap. I guess we've all been pretty lazy . . . lately."

"For real?" said Jasper, peering around the room. "This does *not* look like the house of a lazy family. Everything in the kitchen is so shiny and neat."

"Oh, well, Olga cleans it," I said. "The kitchen and the bathroom, and the floors and stuff, so things don't ever get too gross."

"Wow, you have a maid?" asked Jasper.

"Not a maid exactly," I explained. "Just a lady who comes and mops and vacuums and stuff. Every couple of weeks."

"Where I'm from that's called a maid."

"Well, yeah," I said. "I guess. It's been a new thing this year. We used to have a chore chart. And mostly we kept up with it. Dad did the bathroom. He called himself *King of the Throne*."

Jasper laughed. "That sounds like a dorky TV-show dad thing to say."

"Yeah, maybe," I said. "And Mom did the floors, and I did the dishes and . . . well, anyway we divided it all up. But then things changed. . . ."

"Why?"

I shrugged. "Just, things changed. Mom and Dad started having trouble keeping up with the house. And I tried to help, some. But then I spilled a bottle of shampoo, and tried to vacuum it up, and it turns out you can't vacuum up shampoo. Just in case you ever wondered. . . ."

"Uh, *yeah*," said Jasper, with a grin. She wasn't even trying not to laugh at me, but that was okay. The whole thing had been pretty stupid.

"So now Olga comes," I said with a shrug. "But little things like the lint trap . . . we forget about them, I guess. Everyone has been sort of . . . distracted this year. Olga doesn't do lint traps. Or cat boxes. I hate cleaning the cat box."

"Sure. Who doesn't?" said Jasper as she settled back down onto the couch and snuggled under the blanket. "But cats are nice. I haven't seen yours!"

"He comes and he goes," I said.

I turned the movie back on, and we watched some more, until the dryer buzzed. Then Jasper got up, and I heard her futzing around in the office. She came back in, holding a basket full of laundry to fold. She was wearing shorts and a *Star Wars* T-shirt with Princess Leia on it.

"*Much* better," I said.

"You're telling me," said Jasper. "Hey, while I'm hanging out here anyway, I want to wash my stupid nightshirt, if that's cool. Do you have any laundry to run with it?"

"Sure," I said. "I think so. . . ." I paused the movie again and stood up, yawning.

Jasper followed me to my room, where I scrounged dirty leggings, shorts, and a sundress from the floor and dresser top. "Here, this should make a load," I said. I reached out and took her pink shirt from her, then headed for the office.

I'd just assumed Jasper was following along behind me

down the hall, but as I neared the office door I heard her say, "Hey, mind if I use the facilities?"

"Of course not," I called back, over my shoulder, but when I turned, I realized that Jasper didn't actually know where the bathroom was. "No, wait!" I called out, as she reached out for the knob of a closed door.

But it was already too late. Jasper swung the door wide, and it creaked on its hinges. Like a door nobody had opened in a long time. Like a door that had been sealed up tight for a year.

"Uh," she said, peering in.

"Wrong room," I said. What else could I say?

"Oh," said Jasper. And then she whispered, "Oh, Leah..."

She said it like she already knew. Everything. I joined her, backtracked the few short feet to stand beside her. Clutching my armload of laundry, I stared into the room. For the first time in a long time. For the first time in a year.

It was dark. All the lights were off, and the curtains were closed. Even so, you could make out the layer of dust on everything. Dust and shadows, floating in the air. The room was a memory.

"Olga doesn't clean this room," I said. "Nobody cleans this room."

"I get it," said Jasper somberly.

Now that the door was open, I couldn't look away. I stared around at everything, at the rumpled striped bedspread that had been pulled up quickly, the very last time Mom ever said, "Samuel Aaron Davidson! Are you *sure* you made your bed today?" I took in the low Lego table, covered in half-built robots and starships, and the desk cluttered with junk of all kinds—pipe cleaners and broken chunks of Styrofoam.

Worst of all was the familiar orange backpack, slung over the desk chair, hastily half zipped and abandoned, untouched since the last day of school. How many times had I trudged along behind that stupid backpack? Twice a day, every day, for years. Sam had always been in a hurry. He ran everywhere. I remembered, so clearly, how Dad would bellow after him, at every single intersection, "Full stop, kid! Look both ways!" I hadn't heard Dad raise his voice like that in a long, long time.

When I tore my gaze away from the room, I found Jasper staring at me. Probably waiting for me to undo what she'd done. Make it okay. And I wanted to. I wanted to close the door and go back to five minutes ago, but my arms were full of laundry. I didn't have a free hand.

I opened my mouth. "Jasper, I . . ." but the right words weren't there.

She looked nervous, hesitant.

I cleared my throat. "Jasper," I said again. "Can you please . . ."

"Leah? What is it . . . ?"

I made my voice louder. I tried to make it sound normal.

"It's just . . . I need you to pull the door closed. Can you? My arms are full."

"Oh!" said Jasper, shaking her head. "Of course. Sorry!"

Then she reached out and pulled it shut. She didn't slam it, but she didn't close it softly either, exactly. She closed it with a firm, even click.

Once the door was closed, I found I could move again. My feet came unstuck, and I turned away from Jasper without a word. I left the hallway, headed straight for the office, where I busied myself with shoving the dirty clothes in the washer. I added the soap, measuring more carefully than usual. I pushed the button. I took a breath. I took a few breaths.

When I got back to the living room, Jasper was waiting on the couch. She was holding the clicker and had the red blanket back over her lap, even though she didn't need it anymore to cover herself. Her eyes peered up at me, worried.

I sat down beside her, and she didn't say anything, just spread the red blanket over my legs too, and gave me a funny little pat on my knee. I guessed she felt terrible, but I wasn't mad. Not really. I wasn't really sure exactly *how* I felt. A little bit like I wanted a glass of water. A little bit like I might hiccup.

Finally I turned to her. "Go ahead," I said. "You can ask. It's okay."

"Are you sure?"

I nodded.

"Really?" she said. "Because it seemed very . . . private,

that room. It seemed like a kind of secret."

"It is, I guess," I said, picking at the blanket on my lap. "I don't know why, really. But it is . . . a kind of secret. Even though everyone knows. Can something be a secret if everyone in the whole world knows it? If you just don't talk about it, ever?"

Jasper's eyes were on me—huge and soft and full of questions. But it was okay. I could handle it. Though after a year of definitely *not* being able to handle it, I wasn't sure why I could handle it today. Maybe because she hadn't ever known him. Maybe because she was someone new. And maybe just because she was Jasper.

"You can ask me," I said again softly. "I promise it's okay."

We were silent a minute longer before she opened her mouth. "What was his name?" she asked.

"Sam," I said. Now there were tears in my eyes, but they felt warm and right. Good, even. I could handle this. "His name was Sam."

Jasper blinked, and I could see that she had tears in her eyes too. I was grateful. They made it easier, somehow. Made my tears feel okay. I wiped at my eyes with the ugly orange cuff of my stupid footie pajamas. I was still dressed like a duck. Why was I still dressed like a duck?

"Sam," she said. "*Sam*. It's a nice name."

"Yes," I said. "He was a nice kid. I mean, he was a regular kid. So sometimes he wasn't nice. Sometimes he made me crazy. I guess that's what little brothers do. But mostly he was nice."

"And he . . ."

"He . . . died," I said softly. "Drowned. In a lake. It was . . ." I wanted to keep going, tell her more, but I just couldn't. The words wouldn't come. I opened my mouth and then closed it again. One heavy tear rolled down my cheek. "I . . ."

Suddenly, outside, with no warning at all, a huge crash of thunder exploded and rattled the windows. The living room dimmed, and through that dusky light, Jasper and I peered at each other, side by side on the sofa. The sounds of rain filled the room, a regular spatter on the pavement outside and the sharp plinks and pings of drops hitting the metal roof above the chimney.

I wiped away the tear, and then gave a little laugh. "If it's raining, it must be lunchtime," I said.

"Huh?" said Jasper.

"Oh," I said. "It's an old thing my dad used to say. He swore that summer storms always happened exactly when he was about to leave work for a lunch break. He said it was a curse in Georgia—that it always rains here at the worst possible moments."

"Really?" said Jasper.

"Of course not really," I said. "It was just my dad trying to be funny. He used to be the king of bad jokes. Dorky TV-show dad, like you said."

Jasper didn't laugh. "Leah, I'm sorry I opened that door. . . ."

"It's *really* okay," I said. "I promise."

"No." She shook her head. "I don't think it was. I didn't mean to do that. I never would have. . . ."

"It's really, *really* okay," I said. "It's just a door, Jasper. You opened it. That's what doors are *for*. I think it's actually a good thing. Maybe."

"Seriously?"

I nodded and looked her straight in the eye. "I *swear*, Jasper. I mean it."

"I believe you," she said. "But I'm still sorry."

"You know what?" I said. "I hate it, the secret. If that's what it is. I hate how things are here. I hate the door being shut, and that my mom and dad don't talk about it. Him. Sam. *They're* silent. *They* closed the door, and turned into ghosts. So we don't talk about anything real. I've forgotten how, I think. To talk. Not just to them, but to everyone. At school, I was a ghost too, the last year. Like I floated along and couldn't find a way to speak or be with anyone. It's hard to talk about it, with people who knew him, and also hard *not* to."

"You don't seem like a ghost now," said Jasper.

"The thing is . . . ," I said, "when it happens, *death*, people actually stop making eye contact with you. Did you know that? Your friends, even your best friends. Like with my— with Tess, whose house we walked past, remember?"

Jasper nodded. "Yeah."

"It wasn't like she *wanted* to ditch me. I don't think she meant to do it. It was just like she didn't know how to talk to me anymore. After being friends all our lives. Nobody did, nobody who'd known Sam. Even your teachers stop calling on you in class. It's like they're afraid the sadness could rub off on them, or something. As if that could be true. As if there's any way that talking to someone for a few minutes, and acting normal, could do . . . *this* to a person."

"Wow," she said. "That's . . . a lot."

I nodded again. "Yeah, and then after a while, *you* forget how to make eye contact too. So that when people try, you can't do it anymore. Even people you love, your *best* people. It's awful."

"I can imagine that," said Jasper.

"You know what else? My parents, they even . . ." A few tears rolled free, slid down my cheeks as I glanced at the mantel over the fireplace. I wiped at them quickly. "They even took down his pictures. All of them."

"Why?"

"I guess they just couldn't handle seeing him every day. When he wasn't coming back. I don't know what they did with the photos, but it's killing me. I can't find him anywhere. I can't . . ." I shook my head.

"What?"

"It's like I'm starting to forget his face. I close my eyes, and I can't see him."

Jasper shook her head. "That's terrible, Leah. You don't see a therapist or . . . your rabbi, or anything?"

I shook my head and rubbed my nose. I wasn't looking at her anymore. I didn't mind talking about it, but it felt clunky, uncomfortable. I wasn't sure how to do this.

"We aren't really Jewish like *that*," I said. "We don't really have a rabbi. And I did see a therapist, for a minute," I explained. "For a few weeks, at the beginning. But then Mom and Dad went back to work, and the appointments got hard to schedule. Nobody could drive me, and they had a fight—well, like a tense quiet argument, a conversation, about whether I was old enough to take an Uber alone to the therapist's office. Mom said no and Dad said yes, and I think they just couldn't handle fighting, so they dropped it, and I got a kitten instead."

"No!" said Jasper. "A *cat*? That was their solution? Seriously?"

I nodded, and then I couldn't help it, I smiled a little. Because it sounded so ridiculous. "*Seriously*. But it was actually kind of a good thing, because when people don't talk to you like a normal person anymore, it's nice to have a kitten. To talk to."

Jasper looked horrified. "Tell me they didn't name the kitten after—"

"No!" I said. "Oh, God, no, can you imagine? My parents aren't *that* clueless. The kitten is called Mr. Face. He's a cat now, and he's fine. Mostly he stays outside. But he's fuzzy, and he sleeps with me. I love him."

"Well, kitten or no kitten," said Jasper, "you *should* be seeing someone, Leah. You need to see someone."

"What makes you say that?" I said. "Do you . . . *see someone?*"

"Not . . . just now," said Jasper. "But I know about therapists. Trust me. I could tell you some stories. . . ."

Then she paused. There was a funny look on her face, as she stared out the window, and for a second, I thought she was going to actually *tell* me the stories. Whatever they were. But then she stood and stretched instead.

"Hey," she said. "It seems like the rain is pretty much over. So maybe I should go home before it starts up again. I can just take my nightshirt damp, and let it hang to dry. Cool?"

It wasn't at all. It was the furthest thing from cool. In that moment I wanted to push Jasper back down on the sofa, trap her with the red blanket. I wanted to say that it was fine she had opened the door to Sam's room. I wanted her to know that she didn't have to tell me her stories if she didn't want to. That she could have her secrets, whatever they were. I wanted her to know that it was enough just to sit together and watch movies. I wanted her to stay with me. I didn't want to be alone again.

Instead I nodded. "Cool."

So Jasper ran to grab her nightshirt, and the rest of her laundry, from the office. Then she left, walked out the front door, and down the porch steps. I stood in the doorway and watched her go. Thinking that I hadn't even gotten her number. Why hadn't I gotten her number? But somehow, I couldn't bring myself to call out to her now. It felt wrong, to ask for more.

When Jasper reached the street, she turned back and gave a friendly nod. "Bye, Leah," she called. "And thanks. For everything!"

"Anytime!" I shouted back in the most normal, casual tone I could muster.

But I meant it. Truly. I meant *anytime*. I meant *any time at all, do not hesitate*. I meant *please come back soon and sit with me and talk to me, like I'm still a normal person*. I hoped she knew that, as she turned around and walked away down the street. I watched her fuzzy red hair until she turned onto Hemlock and disappeared from view. Then I stood a little longer, staring at the empty street, at the spot where Jasper had been.

Until suddenly, at my feet, Mr. Face appeared. He popped out of the overgrown azaleas that choked the porch and trotted over to me with a limp mouse hanging from his teeth. He carried the mouse lightly, gently, and when he reached me, he laid the mouse down on the mat at my feet and gave a mew. As if to say, *I know you were talking about me. See, I'm not useless.*

"Thanks," I said to Mr. Face, examining his gift. "Thanks a lot."

I waited there like that for a minute, feeling the muggy poststorm air heat up around me, feeling the steam rising from the sidewalk and the street. I looked at the dead mouse at my feet, and I tried to take it all in. The open door to Sam's room, the insane pajamas I was still wearing, which were way too hot for today, Jasper, and Mr. Face. It felt like a story I was reading or a movie I was watching. There were too many pieces to the story, and I couldn't quite take it all in or make sense of it.

Then Mr. Face turned and darted away, back into the azaleas, and so I reached down to gather up the mat at my feet, with its sad limp mouse. But a strange thing happened.

The mouse woke up.

It gave a little shake, a shudder. Its nose twitched, and a moment later it sat up on its haunches and looked around. I swear that half-dead mouse stared at me.

"Hi," I said, startled.

The mouse blinked.

"Wow," I said. "It's a miracle! I thought you were a goner for sure, little guy."

The mouse didn't answer. It turned and ran off, raced across the porch and jumped between the spindles, then down into the piles of dead leaves that nobody had bothered to rake for a year.

Of course, I knew it wasn't magic that had woken up the

mouse. There was a perfectly reasonable explanation. The mouse hadn't been dead in the first place, only stunned. But it *felt* like magic. Anyway, it felt like something. And maybe just being alive, and a little brown mouse—able to sit up, twitch your nose, dash into the old dry leaves—maybe *that* was magic enough.

THE ACTUAL WORLD

I didn't go back to the farm for a few days after that. I wanted to, badly, in hopes of seeing Jasper there. But when I woke up each morning, I felt too nervous, almost sick to my stomach. I'd said so *much* to Jasper, after not saying anything to anyone for so long. It felt like I'd emptied myself, like I was an eggshell without the egg in it. On top of that, I'd cried, in my too-small ugly yellow footie pajamas, and I felt . . . ridiculous. As badly as I wanted to see Jasper again, I was a little afraid of what would happen when I did. I was so full of feelings. I didn't think I could bear it if she laughed at me.

In one part of my brain—the part that remembered watching *Harry Potter* together, sharing breakfast, laughing and talking and sprawling on the couch—I knew that the day *had* been fun, and easy. But another part of me could only think of how it had ended, with her sudden departure. And so each morning, I stayed in bed for hours, staring at the ceiling, rubbing my nervous belly, and hoping that Jasper might just show up on my doorstep, smiling her big smile, and fix everything.

But of course, after a while, my nervous belly would turn into a hungry belly and growl at me for a bowl of Cheerios. Then I'd get out of bed, eat, take a shower, and pull on some clothes. And once I'd done all that, I was surprised to discover I wanted to *do things*. For the first time in a long time, it wasn't enough to just sit around. I didn't do anything special, really. Just regular everyday things. Like, one day I decided to rake the leaves out of the flower beds in the front yard all by myself, and mow the lawn. It felt good to stretch and sweat, even though I ended up with blisters on both hands. The next day, I swept the porch clean, and watered the few pots of half-dead plants that had been sitting there all year, unattended.

On Thursday, I baked a pan of brownies. I didn't make them from scratch or anything. Just plain old brownies from a box. But I stirred in a handful of chocolate chips and a handful of pecans, and the house filled with the most wonderful smell. I took them out at exactly the right moment, so that they were still a little undercooked and gooey, and I couldn't help thinking how nice it would be if Jasper happened to stop by in time for warm brownies. She didn't. Still, they were perfect. So I sat at the kitchen table, all by myself, and ate two brownies, with a big glass of milk. And after I was done, I decided I was being silly, and worrying too much. If Jasper wasn't going to come for a brownie, I'd have to take the brownies to her.

Carefully, I wrapped up two big squares in tin foil and slipped them into a tote bag. I dug an old sippy cup out of a cabinet, filled it with milk, and snapped on the lid. Then— with a twenty in my pocket, *house rule!*—I left, taping a note to the door as I closed it behind me. I had to write the note out a few times to get it right. I kept accidentally putting in too many exclamation points. At last I ended up with:

> Dear Jasper,
>
> I had to go out for a while, but I want to see you again, and I don't know where you live. I'll stop by the farm, but if you come here, leave me your number or address, or call me (404-555-4447). There's a pencil in the mailbox!
>
> Leah

When I arrived at the farm, there was no sign of Jasper. I searched everywhere I could think of, up the creek and down. I checked the swing and the garden, with no luck. Finally, I stood there, brownies in hand, feeling gloomy, and figured I'd just have to go home.

Then I looked around me. There was the bright green hill of high grass and the red clay bank of the creek. I heard a trilling birdsong I didn't recognize in the trees over my head, and noticed a hill of fire ants, busy at my feet. All around me, the world was happening, and it seemed wrong to go home so soon. *Jasper wouldn't go home, would she?* I thought. And it was true. *What would Jasper do?*

She'd *go* somewhere. She'd *do* something. I wasn't sure what, but *something*. I was sure if it. So I did another thing I hadn't done in a long time: I left the neighborhood. I took Mercer back out to Woodland and started along my usual path, but after a minute, I headed east. I waited at the light and, when it changed, made my way across the four crazy lanes of Moreland Avenue, into East Atlanta Village.

I walked slowly, peering in the windows of all the businesses, where people were talking and shopping and bustling around, and it was fascinating, like watching TV almost. I'd walked this same street a thousand times before, of course, but after weeks alone, everything seemed so busy. The cars passing by felt faster and louder than I remembered them. Each time a door opened and someone stepped out onto the sidewalk from a store or bar, music trailed after them into the street. A different song every time.

As I pulled open the door of the coffee shop, I realized I couldn't remember the last time I'd been to Joe's. I tried to think back, and what I came up with was Sam in this place, with hot chocolate or lemonade, depending on the season. How many times had we sat here together on the worn-out sofa, while Mom ran to the post office or the copy shop? Sam making annoying sounds at his iPad, and me pretending not to know him in case someone I knew came in.

The memory made me wince a little, but I sat with it anyway, until it went away. And then it felt good just to sit under the big ceiling fans, sipping my drink and watching all the people doing the things people do. People typed on laptops and read books. A man in an armchair was knitting, and there was a mom beside me on the couch, whispering into her phone, with a baby asleep on her lap.

After a little while, two high school kids came in and sat down across from me. They pulled out a deck of cards and started to play some complicated game I couldn't follow, but when they caught me staring, one of them smiled at me, and that made me blush. I could feel it. So I finished my mocha quickly, drained the very sweet thick last sip, as I stood up and headed for the counter.

"Thanks, beautiful," said the man at the register when I slid my glass over to him. "You make sure to have a great day, okay?"

It was the first thing anyone had said to me all afternoon, and I wasn't entirely expecting it. But his voice was kind and warm and rich, and his eyes were sort of smiling at me too, crinkling up at the corners in a nice way.

"Oh!" I said. "Thank you. I'll try."

"That's all you can do," he said.

Suddenly, I had an idea. I reached into the tote over my

arm, took out the silver packet of brownies, and set them on the counter. "I made these," I said.

"For me?" said the man.

I nodded.

"Well," he said, "it's my lucky day."

"Mine too," I said with a smile. And though I wasn't sure why, as I left the coffee shop, and heard the bell jingling behind me as the door closed, I had the strangest feeling—almost like a knot that had been tied tightly inside me was suddenly loosening all on its own.

When I got home, it was later than I'd realized, and I found my dad sitting at the kitchen table. He was eating a large brownie and staring absentmindedly at his phone. He glanced up quickly when I opened the door. "Oh, hey, Leah!" he said guiltily. "Don't tell your mom I spoiled my dinner."

I laughed loudly, without meaning to. It just seemed really funny for some reason. My big dad, feeling guilty over a brownie. As if it mattered whether he ate a brownie. "My lips are sealed," I said, grinning at him.

Then he smiled too. "Hey, did *you* make these?" he asked, raising his brownie. "They're really good."

I nodded, wondering where else he thought they could possibly have come from. "Yeah," I said. "I had a craving."

"Well, thanks, sport!" He took another bite, and disappeared back into his phone.

So I headed through the house to the front door, to take down my Jasper note, thinking that I couldn't remember the last time he'd called me *sport*.

The next day, after my usual lazy morning and a late breakfast of cinnamon toast, I decided to head back into East Atlanta again. I thought maybe I'd go to the library after the coffee shop. But this time, as I was heading along Woodland toward Moreland, I looked up and saw a tall thin woman with short brown hair. Inside my chest, there was a sudden rush, a flurry of feathers.

"Bev!" I choked out as we almost bumped into one another. "Hey. How's . . . Tess?"

"Leah, hi," she said. "How are you, sweetie? We haven't seen you in forever. You should stop by the house sometime soon."

"Oh, I . . . well, I guess I've been busy. I didn't know you were back from New York already. That was a quick vacation."

Bev looked confused. "Yes, we just went up for a week this year. We came home early because . . . well, have you not talked to Tess?"

"No," I said. "Is . . . everything okay?"

"Ye—ess," she said slowly.

"So why aren't you staying for a month like usual? Is everything okay?"

72

Bev's forehead was drawn now. She looked like she was working something out. "Of course. Everything's fine. It's only that . . . well, Tess has been saying for years she wanted to go to . . . to camp."

"*Camp?*" That word hit me hard.

She nodded.

"Camp. *My* camp?"

Bev wasn't meeting my eyes, so I knew I was right.

"What camp, Bev?"

"Camp Whippoorwill," she said, and it came out funny, sort of breathy.

"Oh." I said. Then again. "Oh." I couldn't find any more than that. My brain was stumbling.

Now her words tumbled out in a rush. "It's just . . . you always made it sound so wonderful, with the lake and the archery and the plays and everything, and so we booked her early last year, ahead of schedule, thinking you two girls would go together."

"Sure," I said. "That would have been . . . fun."

"And of course, you didn't go back this year, but Tess was really excited, and so it seemed a shame not to let her . . ." Her voice trailed off.

"That makes sense," I said. "Sure." Except that it didn't.

"I'm so sorry, Leah . . . ," she said, looking almost pained. "I assumed you and Tess had talked about this. I thought you knew. I hate to be the one to . . ."

"Yeah," I said. "I could see how you'd think that." In the world where Tess and I were still real friends, where she still talked to me like an actual person, that would have made sense.

"And Leah, I absolutely hate to do this. It's a terrible time to dash. But I'm afraid I'm running late. I'm just rushing down to the school for a board meeting."

"Oh, sure," I said.

Bev shifted her purse on her shoulder, forced a smile. "Well, okay then, Leah. It was so nice to see you, and will you please tell your mom we're home? She should . . . call me."

"Sure," I said.

"We really need to . . . catch up. . . ."

I nodded. "Will do."

To catch up. Like that was the most normal thing in the world. When I was pretty sure that, until this past year, they'd never gone more than a week without seeing each other, for as long as I'd been alive.

"Okay," she said. "Well, thanks. And you should write Tess a letter. I'm sure she'd be excited to get mail at camp."

I just blinked. As she reached down and hugged me tightly, it felt like any other Bev hug, with her chin poking into my shoulder. She meant it, I could tell, but I could feel her heart racing against me, too fast.

Then she ran away. Like, actually *ran.* Which was kind of funny. It isn't often you see a grown-up woman run down a street when they aren't wearing yoga pants and earbuds. I stared after her for a minute before I turned and stumbled off in the other direction. I didn't know what else to do with myself, so I just kept on going, heading to East Atlanta as planned.

It was almost like I was floating along in a fog. I wasn't sure exactly *what* I was feeling. I knew I was angry, but I wasn't sure why. And the anger was mixed with something else. Envy? Sadness? It was all just a big confusing swirl of feelings. I couldn't help picturing Tess at camp, with *my* camp friends, in *my* craft cabin or *my* bunk. Tess even knew about my special reading place, in the oak tree. I wondered if she'd try to find that and take it for herself, along with everything else.

I drifted, lost in all that, toward the noise and traffic of Moreland, only stopping for the red light. But then, standing at the corner, I glanced across the street and saw a familiar profile at the bus stop. She was sitting on the bench, staring down at her phone.

A cloud of red curls.

My confusion suddenly cleared. The fog lifted. My heart jumped. "Jasper! I shouted. "Hey, Jasper!"

I saw her raise her head at the sound of my voice, but at that very moment, the bus pulled up in front of the stop and blocked her from view. If she got on, I'd miss her.

So I looked both ways, into the crazy traffic of Moreland Avenue. I was never allowed to cross here except with the light. Mom and Dad had lectured me to death about it. Once, a man in a wheelchair had been hit at this intersection.

Cars whizzed past me in three lanes as the bus sat on the other side of the road, blocking the fourth lane. But suddenly, a gap appeared, a magical empty lull. And for a strange hushed moment, there was no traffic at all. It was as if the universe had made a space for me. Exactly the space I needed. So I took my shot and dashed across.

I darted around the bus and found that, sure enough, Jasper was no longer sitting on the bench. The bench was empty, except for somebody's McDonald's trash, crumpled and abandoned. But the bus door was still open, yawning like a cave, waiting for me.

With no thought at all, I hopped up and on.

ALL SETTLED

"Hi!" I said to the bus driver, climbing three very large steps.

"Hey," he called back as he leaned down to pull some kind of lever that closed the door. "You almost missed me!"

I peered down the length of the bus, at a bunch of strangers who didn't seem remotely interested in me, and there at the back sat Jasper, staring out the window, craning her neck and looking around. For me?

"Jasper!"

She turned her head, saw me, grinned, and waved. A bunch of passengers stared up at me too. But they didn't look friendly. Then I realized that while I'd been focused on Jasper, the driver had been mumbling at me. Now he was waiting for something, but I didn't know what.

"Oh!" I said. "Sorry. Can you say that again? I didn't catch it."

"I *said*," the driver growled, "do you plan to pay me, so we can leave?"

"I—of course!" I stammered. "How much is it?"

"Two fifty," he said, staring not at me now but through the windshield and out into the street. Clearly annoyed.

I fumbled in my pocket and pulled out the twenty I'd brought with me, held it out to him. "Here," I said. "I have money!"

"Can't make change," said the driver, glancing briefly at the cash.

"Huh?"

"I said I can't make change. Bus can't make change. Got it?"

I looked back over my shoulder, past all the other riders at Jasper, who had scooted over to make room for me on the seat beside her. She was waiting, grinning.

"But that's all my money," I said. "How will I get home?"

The bus driver rolled his eyes. "Call your mommy."

It didn't seem fair at all. But Jasper was waiting, and that mattered more than twenty dollars, or it felt like it did anyway. So I said, "Okay, I guess," and the driver—still with his eyes on the road, plucked the bill neatly from my fingers.

The bus jerked to life as I made my way to the back of the bus, and when it picked up speed I found myself sort of stumbling and flying toward Jasper. I nearly landed in her lap.

"Hey!" I said, when I slid into the seat beside her. "Fancy meeting you here!"

"Crazy!" she said. "Where are you going?"

"Actually," I said, "I was just walking into the village . . . but I've been wanting to see you. And I'm having kind of a strange day already. So when I spotted you there at the bus stop, I guess I just . . . hopped on too. Is that weird?"

She stared at me for a second. Then she burst out laughing. "Yes!" she said. "Yes, Leah, it is absolutely totally bizarre that you jumped on a bus behind me without thinking about it. But it makes me happy, so who cares if it's weird? I've been wanting to see you too."

She meant it, I could tell. I sighed and sank back into the seat.

"Well, if you've been wanting to see me, why didn't you come visit?" I asked. "You can stop by anytime."

Jasper shrugged and looked away from me, out the window beside her. "Oh, you know," she said.

"I *don't*, actually," I said. Now that Jasper was staring out the window, I found myself gazing straight ahead of me, into the back of an old lady's hat. The hat was purple. "I thought we had fun the other day," I said, to the hat.

"We did!" said Jasper. "Of course we did, silly."

"I even left you a note when I went out. I was hoping you'd come by and find it."

Jasper sighed.

"Sorry!" I said. "I'm sorry. I sound pathetic right now. I don't mean to. Don't be mad. It's fine."

"*Mad?*" she said. "I'm not mad, Leah. I just felt like . . ."

"Like what?"

"Like *I* was the pathetic one. Eating all your food and washing my clothes and watching your TV in your fancy house. You were so nice, and *I* was the needy one, not you."

"That's not true," I said. "Not at all!"

Jasper shook her head. "And *then*, after you were so generous, there I went, opening that door, and asking you all those questions. About . . . your brother. Like the clumsiest person in the world. I didn't come back because I was embarrassed I'd been so rude. And because I didn't want you to think I was some kind of leech. I didn't want you to think I was using you."

It took me a minute to process what she was saying. *She'd* been nervous? *She'd* felt weird? *She'd* been trying to be careful? All that added up to was that she cared.

"This is stupid," I said. "We're both being stupid."

Jasper nodded. "Agreed."

"Look," I said, "I am going to tell you the very big true thing, and if it's too weird, you can ride away into the sunset and never talk to me again, okay? But please don't laugh?"

"I promise."

I took a deep breath and said, "Ever since my brother died, I have been lonely and it has been awful and I haven't known how to make it better. I haven't had any clue how to begin."

"Well, sure," said Jasper. "It sounds incredibly hard."

"Yeah, but, like, lonely in a *really* bad way. *All* alone. Like I told you before, everyone has been weird with me. Even Tess. We'd walk to school each day together like always. Not really talking. We'd eat lunch at our usual table. But only eating. Like strangers. After being friends all our lives. And then my parents . . ." I took a breath.

"I'm so sorry," Jasper said.

"No, don't be!" I said. "Really, don't. Because last week, with *you*, I had fun, and felt okay, and normal. Normal for the first time in a year."

"I'm glad," said Jasper. "That's good, right?"

"Right," I said. "Of *course* it's good. But the thing is . . . it felt so good that all I have thought about since then is seeing you again. Hoping that maybe I can feel normal more often. Maybe someday, I can even feel normal all the time again. You see? I felt . . . hopeful. Like maybe I wasn't going to be totally a mess forever."

Jasper nodded.

"So the truth is that you can come over anytime you want, and I will never mind, I swear. Not ever. You are my favorite person in the world right now, even though I just met you and

I don't even know you." Then I stopped a moment, because it was like I could hear an echo of my own words inside my head. *I don't even know you.*

"Is that *sad?*" I asked.

Jasper was looking at me now, staring right at me. Intently. "Yes, Leah," she said quietly. "It *is* sad."

I shrugged. "Sorry," I said.

"No, dummy," said Jasper, flipping around to face me fully on the plastic seat. "Not sad in a way you should be sorry for. Sad in a way that means I wish you could feel better."

"Oh," I said.

"Leah," said Jasper. "Your brother died. It's just sad. Of course it's sad. How could anything *not* be sad? If you weren't sad, you'd have to be a crazy person."

I shrugged again. No one had said that to me before.

"Okay, now, is it my turn to talk?" she asked.

"Sure," I said. "I mean, if you want to. . . ."

Jasper grinned and took *her* deep breath. "Look," she said, "I am the new girl and I don't know anyone, and I spend all my time alone too. Hanging out with you was the best time I've had in forever. . . ."

"I'm glad!" I said, smiling.

"Yeah, I know," said Jasper. "And I'm grateful you were so nice to me. But it's more complicated than that, and I'm, well, I don't have much money."

"That doesn't matter!" I said, shaking my head.

"Except that it really does," said Jasper, staring me evenly in the eyes. "And it makes me feel terrible when people have to help me, and you helped me, and so I didn't want to see you again."

"Oh!"

"Only because I didn't want you to be always helping me, and feeling sorry for me. Get it?"

"I do," I said. "Or I think I do. But please, please don't stay away? You can *have* our TV for all I care. I will never mind sharing or helping. I will never feel like that. I mean it. I know it."

"It's nice of you to say that," said Jasper. "But my situation is . . . more complicated than I can explain."

I shook my head. "I don't care. I don't care at all, whatever it is."

Jasper stared at me, and there was a long strained pause. I thought she might tell me what the "situation" was then, and maybe she was considering it, but in the end she just gave a quick nod and said, "Okay, deal!" and stuck out her hand.

So I shook it and said, "Deal!"

Then Jasper laughed and said, "Wow, we are a couple of total freaks, huh?" And I was about to agree with her, but at that very minute the bus stopped and shuddered as the door opened at the front, and Jasper glanced out the window and said, "Oh, this is my stop!"

So I decided to stop worrying and just embrace the

freakiness of everything. "Then I guess it's my stop too!" I said.

Jasper grinned. "Good!" she said. "That's all settled. And you can help me carry the groceries."

Which was a very nice answer. I had never wanted to carry groceries so badly in all my life.

A CERTAIN AMOUNT
OF POWER

As I hopped up to follow Jasper, I realized I had absolutely no idea where the bus had taken us. I'd been so focused on our conversation that even when I'd been gazing out the window, it was more like I was gazing *at* it. Now, as I stepped onto the cracked sidewalk, I looked around myself and knew immediately where we were.

We were way farther down on Moreland than I usually went. Once or twice a year, when Dad suddenly had what he called "a hankering for a real taco," he'd drive us this way and order dinner in fumbling Spanish from a bright orange shack. But we hadn't done that in a long time, and anyway, I hadn't known there was a grocery store this way. We were miles from the Publix or the Kroger.

As I followed Jasper across the sea of dingy parking lot, she explained the plan. "Okay," she said. "So the deal is that I try to get things at the Dollar Tree. If they don't have what I need, we can try the Family Dollar, but those are more expensive, and we have to walk a ways."

"Makes sense," I said. I hated to admit that the dollar stores were all the same to me. That I'd never set foot in any of them, even though they were only a few miles from the house where I'd spent my entire life.

As it turned out, they had everything on Jasper's little list at the Dollar Tree. Peanut butter and granola bars and crackers and applesauce and roach powder and canned vegetable soup and SpaghettiOs and corn and bottles of apple juice and chili and sour gummy worms.

"Your mom sent you to the store to get gummy worms?" I asked, trying not to notice the roach powder.

Jasper laughed. "When you do the shopping, you wield a certain amount of power over your grocery list."

"Good point," I said. "We never buy candy. Maybe I should see if I can help out a little more with the shopping myself."

"Like you helped with the vacuum and the shampoo that time?" asked Jasper, raising her eyebrows.

"Ha. Fair point," I said.

As I strolled around the store, I was amazed at what they had there. Fourth of July decorations that lit up and silk flower wreathes for the door and shoes for kids and the big shiny helium balloons my parents had always said were a waste of money. But everything was somehow only a dollar.

"Why do people pay more at other stores if this stuff is all so cheap?" I said, fingering a packet of really cute penguin stickers and wishing I had money to spend.

"You tell me!" said Jasper.

At the checkout, Jasper magically produced two cloth tote bags from her pocket and loaded all her stuff in. Then she handed me one of the full bags and headed straight next door into a giant secondhand shop that looked like it had once been a big grocery store. It was hard to keep up with her. All those cans really weighed down my bag.

"What do you need here?" I asked, as I stepped inside and nearly bumped into a naked mannequin with no head.

"You'll see," said Jasper mysteriously, heading off into a rack of clothes.

"Men's jeans?" I asked, hurrying behind her.

But Jasper wasn't trying on the pants. Instead she shoved her groceries at me and said, "Here, hold this for a minute," and then she busied herself reaching into the pockets of each pair of pants, moving down the line quickly.

"What are you doing?" I asked.

She didn't reply and I felt like I should understand, but I didn't, not until she glanced up at me with a sneaky grin and I saw something flashing in her fingers. A quarter, glinting silver in the weird fluorescent lights.

"Oh my god!" I shouted. "You're brilliant."

"Shhh," said Jasper. "Just look busy."

As I watched, Jasper went quickly down the rack, nimble fingers pawing at each pocket in turn. When we got to the end of the aisle, we doubled back along the other side of the row. After a bit, I decided to try my own luck, heading over for the winter coats, where I set down my bag of groceries and got to work. I turned up lint and dust, a few staples, and a button or two, but nothing more—until, in the women's purses, I hit the jackpot. Two crumpled dollars in a hidden inside pocket. I couldn't keep myself from squealing, just a little. It felt like we were berry picking or on some sort of scavenger hunt.

For maybe a half hour, both of us crisscrossed the store, weaving past each other occasionally, moving up and down every rack, until finally we met at the front of the store. Me with my two dollars and a pretty rhinestone button, and Jasper with a secret smile. "Okay, let's go," she said.

On the curb a few storefronts down, Jasper sat, and I joined her on the hot pavement beneath the overhang of a tattered awning. "I found two dollars and a button," I said proudly, holding out my cupped hands.

"Hmmm," said Jasper. "Two bucks is great. But I think the button is . . . questionable. You probably shouldn't have taken that."

"What do you mean?" I asked.

"Well," she said, "my thinking has always been that a store

can't charge for money, right? Because they can't sell it. So, like, if I bought a two-dollar skirt, and it had a hundred-dollar bill in it, it would still cost two dollars. If one of the folks who worked there found the money before I did, I'm sure *they'd* pocket it too. But the button is sort of a *thing*. Like, they sell buttons at the store. So if someone found the button, they wouldn't keep it. They'd put it in the button box and sell it for a quarter. Know what I mean?"

I didn't understand. "So you think you might get in more trouble for the button than the cash?"

"No," she said thoughtfully. "It's not that. Honestly, they're not going to call the cops over pocket change. The folks who work there probably do it too. It's more like . . . a code."

"A code?" I said.

"Just, rules to live by," she said. "It's weird. But I feel like somehow the button is theirs, and the money is ours. I'm not sure why it matters to have rules, but it does matter. To me. Make sense?"

"I guess so," I said. I wasn't sure that it did make sense, actually. But I nodded anyway. This was Jasper's adventure. I was just trailing along behind her, soaking everything up. It made sense to me that we followed her code, whatever that meant. Especially since I wasn't sure that I even had a code. *Did* I have a code?

"Okay," I said. "I'll remember next time."

"Cool," she said, with a nod. "Thanks!"

"So, what'd *you* find?" I asked.

With a special extra-secret smile, Jasper opened her hand and unfolded it, and in the center of her palm was some change. Quarters and dimes. But shining on top was a silver dollar. "Look!" she said.

"Oh, neat," I said. And it *was* neat, but not as neat as Jasper's smile.

"I love silver dollars," she said, running her finger over the shiny surface. "They're my favorite. Have you had one before?" She held it out for me to inspect, like it was a talisman of some kind, a rare jewel.

I thought about all the silver dollars I'd gotten from the tooth fairy over the years, and the ones Sam had too. It was a tradition at our house. "Yeah," I said. "I have, a few times . . . but why do you like them so much?"

Jasper shrugged. "I don't know. Because they last forever? And because they're prettier than they have to be. And people forget about them. They spend them like quarters, without realizing. Silver dollars just feel . . . special. Different from regular money. You know?"

Suddenly I *did*. As I stared at the coin shining in Jasper's upturned palm, that silver dollar seemed like the most special thing in the world. So special I had a lump in my throat, though I wasn't exactly sure why.

"Anyway, come on!" said Jasper, handing me a gummy worm. "It's been a good day. Let's get over to the bus stop."

"Oh, before we do that," I said, "I have to tell you something. I had a problem on the bus, before, and I guess now I need to borrow fifty cents."

"What do you mean?" asked Jasper. "I mean, sure, you can borrow the money, but what happened on the bus?"

"Well, see . . . I didn't have exact fare when I got on the bus to come here, and I didn't know the driver couldn't make change, so . . ."

Jasper stared at me. "Leah! You're kidding me. How much did you pay to ride the bus?"

I cringed. Thinking of how hard we'd each worked for a few dollars just now, and how far we'd ridden to save money on peanut butter only made it harder to spit out the words. "Twenty dollars."

"TWENTY DOLLARS!" Jasper looked furious.

"I'm sorry," I said. "I'm sorry, I know, it's so dumb. I'm dumb. I only had a twenty. It's a rule of my dad's that I always have a twenty for cab fare if I need it. My dad doesn't take the bus. . . ."

"Don't apologize," said Jasper. "I'm not angry at you. Why do you always feel guilty when you should be mad? You got ripped off!"

"But he said he couldn't make change."

"Well, maybe technically, he doesn't have to. But anyone else on that bus would have broken the twenty if they could. And *I* was right there myself and would have helped if you'd asked. Any decent bus driver will help you out when that happens. Haven't you ever ridden the bus?"

I shook my head, oddly embarrassed not to have done something I'd never even thought about doing until today.

Suddenly Jasper was walking fast and I was walking behind her, and she looked mad but also kind of on fire and excited, and I wasn't sure what was going to happen next.

"Do we . . . ," I called out from behind, "do we walk home now?" It was about three miles, I figured.

"No way," said Jasper. "This route is a straight shot, up and back. That same guy should be driving the next bus or one after that, unless his shift ended. We're going to find him."

In my belly I felt a nervous tremble, but it was also a thrilling feeling. Jasper was in charge. Jasper could handle it. She could handle anything. I'd never known anyone like her in my life, kid or adult. How did she know all the things she knew? She couldn't be that much older than me, but it was like she'd memorized some mysterious handbook that I'd never seen before.

When the bus did pull up, we were in luck. It was the very same driver, with his thick gray mustache and tinted glasses. He looked at us, and if he remembered me, it didn't register on his face. Not at first, anyway.

Jasper climbed up, and I followed her, a little nervous, but eager to see what would happen next.

"Sir?" said Jasper, leaning forward to talk to the driver.

He looked back over his shoulder. "Yes, little lady?"

"My friend here says she gave you a twenty earlier for a single fare," said Jasper as she slid some kind of card through the machine by the driver.

"I don't recall as she did," said the bus driver.

"Oh, really?" said Jasper.

"Nope," said the driver.

"Okay, then," said Jasper. "I thought it would just be easier for you to give her the money back. She has the exact change now and can pay for the ride. But we can call and talk to your manager if you want, and request it formally. If you just want to tell us your name, so we can report you . . ."

Now the bus driver sat up straight, suddenly alert. "Aw, come on, girl. . . ."

"I sure do hope there's a twenty in the box," continued Jasper, "so you don't get in trouble. I mean, if you pocketed the money, and it *isn't* there . . ."

We were holding up the bus now, and time seemed to stretch out unbearably. I could feel eyes all over me. They made me itch, and I wanted to turn and apologize to everyone sitting there, waiting. The woman with the sleeping baby and the man in the janitor's uniform. But Jasper didn't seem to mind at all. She didn't apologize for anything. She just stood there, like no one would be able to move her. Her feet planted.

The driver glanced from Jasper to me, and then back to

Jasper. Finally he sighed and said, "Just sit down. I'll get with you in a minute."

Jasper shot me a grin. Then we stumbled to the first empty row, where we sat down fast as the bus began to move. I was still afraid to breathe normally, but Jasper was beaming, like she'd won a major award.

We rode the whole way in silence. Jasper was watching the driver like a hawk, and I was watching Jasper. But when we got to our stop, and walked past him on our way back to the door, the driver reached up and held out my twenty.

"No hard feelings?" he said.

"No hard feelings," I replied, trying to sound normal and loose, like Jasper, as I plucked the bill from between his fingers.

Then he looked over at Jasper, and said, "Girl, you're a tough one. I pity the man who marries you."

For some reason, when she heard that, Jasper looked back at me and burst out laughing. And then I was laughing too, and I couldn't stop. We both waved goodbye to the puzzled driver, stepped off the bus, and fell straight down to the ground, right there on the scruffy grass beside the cracked sidewalk along Moreland. Then we sat, rocking on our knees, laughing and laughing, grocery bags spilling all around us.

COMPLICATED

O nce we'd recovered, the two of us stood up and started walking, back in the direction of my house, bags slung over our shoulders. But when we got to my street, Jasper stopped walking and turned, reached out a hand. "Can I have my groceries?" she said. "I think this is where we part ways."

"Oh!" I said. "No. That's silly. I'll carry it. I can walk you home, and that way I'll know where you live."

"Nah," said Jasper. "They aren't that heavy, and it's kind of far. Plus, then *you'll* just end up walking home alone."

"Or I can walk you, and then you can walk me, and then I can walk you," I said, grinning. "We can spend all afternoon walking each other home. Back and forth."

But Jasper wasn't grinning. "Please, Leah," she said, with

serious eyes. "Please, just let it go."

"But why? What's the big deal?"

She looked down at her feet. "I don't want you to see where I live," she said softly. "Okay?"

I shook my head. "No," I said. "I don't care what your house looks like. And anyway, we agreed not to worry about that stuff, didn't we? To just be friends? Freaks together. Right?" I smiled.

Jasper wasn't smiling. She only stood, staring at me for what felt like a long minute. I stared right back at her. I *wasn't* going to give up this time.

"Leah, please?" Her voice sounded strained, or maybe tired.

I shook my head. I stood firm. "Nope."

It didn't feel like me at all, this stubbornness. It wasn't a thing I'd ever done, to insist on anything this way. But I wasn't feeling quite like myself. I was a different me suddenly. Blunt. Honest. I wanted to know Jasper, more than I could remember wanting anything. It felt like I *needed* to know Jasper. I didn't like the feeling that she could drift away from me again. That she could disappear. I thought about her leaving, and how I would then just fall back into my silent house, and go back to sleep, with the shadows and the silences; and I knew I didn't want that to happen. I *needed* that not to happen. So I stared at her, silent. Waiting.

She looked down at her feet in their flip-flops, so I looked at her feet too. They were a mess. Her toes were filthy, grubby from the bus and the streets. Orange nail polish chipped and grown out. They were sad toes.

"We could paint our nails," I offered. "At your house. I could paint yours and you could paint mine? It'll be fun."

"You don't understand," said Jasper, turning away from me, walking away from me. "You really don't. I don't know why you're doing this. It will change everything."

But she was wrong. Nothing could change me wanting to be her friend. And I was tired of waiting. Something inside me needed to know more. So I followed her, even though I could tell she was upset. I shifted the strap of the grocery bag higher onto my shoulder, and winced as it cut into the skin under my T-shirt.

Then silently I followed her along Woodland for a few blocks, and I was surprised when she turned onto the rocky gravel of Mercer, back toward the farm, where we'd first met.

"Mercer? But I know everyone who lives on this street!" I said, running to catch up to her. "And I thought you said you lived farther away."

Jasper didn't answer me. She just kept walking. So I followed along silently, kicking gravel. I didn't say anything when we entered the farm. I didn't say anything when Jasper headed down toward the creek and straight into the kudzu jungle, through the scratchy green tendrils that raked at my arms and legs. I was silent as I watched her stomp along the creek. Then she came to a wall of vines and stopped.

She lifted aside a sort of curtain, a veil of vines, to reveal a gap in the green. Through that gap Jasper crawled, and I followed as she scrambled up an embankment overhanging the creek. I had no idea where we were going, but I pushed my own way through and clawed at the red clay and tree roots, trying to keep up, the heavy bag dragging at my shoulder.

A moment later, I burst through all that green, through the kudzu and ivy and honeysuckle, and found Jasper standing in front of a tiny house I'd never seen before. A house I'd never noticed. It was tucked way back in the trees at the edge of the farm, buried in all the vines, pines, and shrubs. I could barely make out the weathered tan color of the clapboards, so overgrown it was in green. Situated like that, the house was blocked from view on all sides, hidden and buried in overgrowth. It was a cottage, really, a tiny miniature house, obviously abandoned and neglected. But it had gingerbread trim and broken stained glass set into the windows. I could tell it had been beautiful once, like something from a fairy tale. But vacated long ago by the elves or hobbits or fauns who had once lived there.

A bright blue dragonfly zipped past my head, and I ducked, startled, almost lost my balance. "Wh—where are we?" I stammered.

"This is where I sleep," said Jasper, turning to face me.

And for just a moment as I stood, facing Jasper—staring at her red hair blazing in the sun with the strange cottage behind her, all covered in vines—she seemed to shimmer, like she would disappear if I didn't keep looking at her. That was silly, of course, but I couldn't help thinking it. For a moment it seemed possible. As if all the childish fantasies I'd ever made up in my life, all the hunger I'd felt for something I couldn't explain, came welling up inside me.

"*This* is your house?" I said.

My mind was reeling, struggling to catch up with the moment, just as my body had struggled to catch up with Jasper's long strides.

"No," said Jasper. "This isn't my house. I . . . don't have a house, at the moment. This is just where I sleep. Temporarily. Do you see now?"

"But . . ."

"I told you it was complicated," she said, shaking her head. "It's *super* complicated."

"But your mom? She lets you just . . ."

Jasper laughed a sad laugh. "Ha, yeah. My mom is complicated too."

I didn't say anything after that. I looked at the little house, and then at Jasper, and then down at the bag of groceries over my shoulder. Trying to take it all in, to understand.

"See? You *didn't* want to know," she said.

But she was wrong about that. She was absolutely wrong about that. And so I shook my head. "Of course I wanted to know," I said. "I'm your *friend*."

"Really?" Jasper glanced up, met my eyes with hers. She looked shy, maybe for the first time since I'd met her. "It's not . . . too much?"

"It's not," I said. "It's a lot. But not too much. It's just confusing. Maybe if you could tell me *why* you—"

But Jasper shook her head then, hard and quick. "Please, no. I can't. I really can't."

"Well, okay," I said. "That's fine. You can tell me or not tell me. Whatever you need to do. But either way, maybe I can help, somehow. . . ."

"You know I don't like help," Jasper said. But she was smiling, just the faintest smile.

"I know it," I said. "But I guess that's just too bad for you. Because it turns out I like helping. *So there*."

"Well," she said with a shrug, "in that case, I guess you might as well come in." She headed for the tall grass on the right side of the house, lifting her knees high, stomping her way to the back door of the house. I followed, stomping behind her.

As I tiptoed into the dim room through the peeling door-frame and stepped into the kitchen of the little worn-out house, as I breathed in the dust and stared up at the ancient cobwebs near the ceiling, as I stood there in the summer heat, I had the strangest feeling the place was somehow familiar. Like a room I'd visited long ago, or maybe dreamed about. Like a room from a book I'd read and forgotten.

There were old fixtures on a white enamel sink, a rusted blue refrigerator, and dingy wooden cabinets. On the floor, a narrow mattress in the corner was draped with a sheet. It was a sad room. But it wasn't *only* that. Because it was also Jasper's room. I looked at her, standing beside a cracked and filthy pane of glass. Her red hair gleamed in the light from the window, despite the dirt.

When I reached up and flipped the switch beside me on the wall, no lights came on, and Jasper shrugged. "Sorry, no power."

"It's okay," I said.

That was a lie. It was *not* okay. It was everything *but* okay that Jasper was living here, like this, alone, with no way to turn on a light.

Jasper didn't want help, but maybe she needed it. She needed someone.

I thought maybe I could be someone.

Without another word, I set down my bag and ran home.

A SOFTER SORT OF HUM

When I ducked back into the house an hour later, Jasper was sitting on the one sad kitchen chair, eating peanut butter from a plastic spoon. Her back was to me, and the filthy broken windowpane still scattered bits of sunlight in her hair. She was just sitting there, licking her spoon, not doing anything else. She turned when she heard the door creak.

"Where did you go?" she asked. "I was beginning to wonder if maybe it was a mistake, bringing you to see all this."

"It wasn't," I said. "Not even a little bit. Sorry if you thought that. I just wanted to run and grab some stuff, and I knew that if I told you that, you'd say you were fine and didn't need anything, but you totally do, and see? I brought . . . *this.*"

I swung my backpack around onto the floor beside me, and

it hit the ground with a thunk. It was a big bag, a navy blue camping pack Dad had used in college. It was dingy and faded and spattered with paint. One of the straps was broken. Every time we cleaned out the closets, Mom threatened to throw it away, but Dad had refused to let her. "My misspent youth is in that bag," he'd said to her, more than once. "It's full of stories the kids aren't ready for yet. But someday, when they're older, they'll want to hear about the year I studied art in Paris, and then hiked across Europe with that banjo player and his dog, don't you think?"

Then Mom would roll her eyes and storm out, and Sam and I would look at each other and nod, because we *did* want to hear those stories.

One time, when Mom had suggested we donate the bag to Goodwill, Dad had actually growled at her. "Argh!" he'd said. "How can you suggest such a thing, you unsentimental woman? Don't you remember that one misty night, on the mountain above Chattanooga?"

He'd raised his eyebrows at her, and Mom had blushed and left the room, shouting, "What am I going to do with you, Paul Davidson!"

Dad had shoved the bag back into the closet then and winked at me. "You never know," he'd said. "Someone might need this good old bag again someday."

And now, at last, someone did.

I crouched down beside it, unbuckled the top, and began

to unpack everything I'd brought with me. Cans and bottles. Bags and jars. They spread and rolled out onto the floor around me.

"I know it looks like a weird bunch of stuff," I said without looking up. "But there's a method to my madness. I promise."

Jasper leaned over from her chair to see what I was doing as I attempted to untangle a long strand of lights that had gotten caught on the lining of the bag. She shook her head at me. "Nice idea," she said. "But I told you, I don't have power."

"Not so fast," I said in triumph as the little solar panel came free from the bag. "Check *this* out."

"Oooooooh," said Jasper. She set down her spoon.

"Right?" I said. "We were going to decorate our back deck with these last summer. But it never happened, and they've been living in a desk drawer ever since. The trick will just be to put the solar panel somewhere it can get light, but then make sure the bulbs are somewhere nobody can see them through the windows if they happen to walk past."

"Wow," said Jasper. "I underestimated you, Leah. You're a serious sneak, huh?"

"I read a lot of books," I explained. "You know, about kids having adventures and stuff? I've sort of been training for this moment all my life. But I guess every kid fantasizes about running away from home, and . . ."

"No, Jasper said firmly. "They don't."

At the sound of her voice, I glanced up from my tangle of lights. "Huh?"

"Kids who might have to do it don't *fantasize* about it at all. They *plan*."

"Oh," I said. "Yeah. That . . . makes sense. Sorry."

I was so curious about *why* Jasper was here. I wanted that story. I could feel it in my belly, like an actual hunger. But she'd made it clear I shouldn't ask her. So I only looked back down at the lights, pretended to unsnarl a knot I'd already loosened.

"It's okay," said Jasper softly. "I got what you meant, and the lights—they're perfect. Thank you."

After that, we fell into a frenzy of cleaning, organizing, and prettying up. The room was sweltering, and the first thing I did was to try to open a window, but they were all swollen shut, so I didn't say anything about the heat, just wiped the beads of sweat from my lip and kept going. It's funny how being a little bit hot can be uncomfortable, but somehow, being super sweaty can be kind of okay, especially when you're working hard, or running, or something like that. Like sweat is different when you earn it.

Using the spray bottle of cleanser and the paper towels I'd brought from home, Jasper and I scrubbed every inch of that kitchen, which was really the only room she seemed to be using. With a broken broom we found in a closet, we swept all the debris and dirt out the back door and right into a bush.

Together, we dragged the bed into the yard, where we gulped fresh air and whacked at the mattress with sticks until it was as clean as it was going to be. Then we dragged it back inside and made it up with a fresh set of too-large sheets and a sky-blue blanket stolen from the linen closet at my house. Carefully, gently, I tucked the blanket under the mattress just so. Much more neatly than I ever made my own bed.

Once the place was clean, we decorated. Jasper spread Mom's old flowered tablecloth on the rickety table, and that brightened things up right away. Just beyond the back door, I set out the little solar panel and then carefully threaded the lights along the floor, snaking them through the kitchen and out into the hallway, so that they reached nearly to the tiny bathroom. Together we arranged the other things I'd brought with me on the kitchen counter—a flashlight, bug spray, candles and matches, extra batteries, and a strange assortment of foods. Jasper laughed as she pawed through the groceries I'd brought. Saltines and Nutella and several jars of pickles. A six-pack of fancy root beer in brown glass bottles, and a box of Cheerios. A packet of Oreos and three peaches. Right away she opened a jar of pickles with a satisfying pop and shoved two in her mouth. "Mmmmm, pickles," she said. "I haven't had a dill pickle in ages." She licked her fingers.

"Interesting," I said. "You went for the pickles first. I would have guessed the Oreos."

"Nah," she said. "You have to eat your dinner before your dessert. Right?"

"Oh, right, dinner!" I said, and pulled out my phone to check the time. I was lucky. It was only 4:50. Mom and Dad weren't even home yet. I thought a second before texting.

Hey Mom. I got invited to dinner at a friend's house. Can I stay? PLEASE?

It only took about two seconds to get a reply:

A playdate! How GREAT! Sure. BE HOME BY DARK!

I groaned faintly at the word *playdate* but didn't say anything to Jasper. Just texted back.

THANKS!

"Sorry," I said. "Just needed to check in with my mom. I didn't know how late it had gotten. But she says I can stay. For dinner."

Jasper laughed and raised the pickle jar. "Well, then," she said, "let's have dinner."

Standing there, pickle in hand, I glanced around at the room, which was a different place altogether now. Cozy. A home. It gave me a little swell of joy, to see the difference I'd made. "I know you didn't want help," I said. "That you don't like when people—"

Jasper rolled her eyes. "Pshhh. Please, I'm over it," she said. "At least for now. Because look at this place . . . and also . . . in case you've forgotten, PICKLES. Have another!"

With a laugh, I took another pickle. Then we munched

for a minute and stared at the newly cleaned kitchen. It was still old and small, but now it was ours, mine and Jasper's. It felt like there was nobody else in the entire world beyond this room. Just us, in this secret place. We could hide here forever, and nobody would know. There would be no weird silences here, or funny glances. No shadows or ghosts. I took a deep breath of the hot, musty air and smiled.

When the pickles were all gone and Jasper had poured the juice down the sink drain, I had one final thought. I went outside and picked a big bouquet of roses from the old bush beyond the door. I got pricked a bunch, but I didn't mind. The dark red petals smelled wonderful, heavy and rich and sweet. I went back inside and set them in the empty pickle jar.

"There," I said. "Is there water in the sink?"

"Nope."

"What have you been doing for showers and tooth brushing and stuff like that? What have you been doing when you need to use the bathroom?"

I guess Jasper could read my face, because she shook her head and laughed. "Don't worry, it's not *that* bad. I haven't been pooping in the creek or anything. There's a hose at the farm, and I fill a jug once a day. I keep it in the bathroom. If you just pour it into the toilet after you go, the toilet sort of flushes itself. I'm not exactly sure how. Something to do with gravity, I guess."

"Really?"

"Yeah."

"Wow, how'd you learn *that*? You just guessed?"

Jasper shook her head. "Someone must have shown me when I was little. I guess the fact that you didn't know it means you've never had your water cut off before."

"No," I said. "I guess I haven't."

"Stick with me and I'll teach you all kinds of useful things," she said. Then she walked off toward the bathroom and returned with the plastic jug full of water. She poured some of it into the pickle jar of roses and set the bouquet on the table.

After that, there was nothing more to do, really, inside the kitchen. As much as I loved the new room, we were both sweating pretty hard, so Jasper and I grabbed two root beers, stepped back outside, and walked around to the front of the house, to the little overgrown porch. The front door was padlocked, and parts of the wooden floor in front of it had fallen away, but the steps were made of concrete, and it was nice and shady there on the stoop, beneath the kudzu hanging off the roof.

We brushed fallen leaves off the steps and sat. Jasper took the top step and I sat below her. Then we drank our root beer, and after a while, the cicadas started up, with their crazy loud chirping buzzing noises, which came in waves, louder for a bit, then subsiding into a softer sort of hum. It was calm, and it felt good to have worked hard with Jasper, to have helped. There was dirt all over me, and cobwebs in my hair, but I didn't care.

"What a day!" said Jasper.

"Has it only been a day? It feels like longer to me. Like I've been here a week." And it really did. As if time had slipped. As if hours spent with Jasper took longer than regular hours, counted for more. Like dog years.

Jasper laughed. "If you'd been here a week, someone would have come looking for you."

"Yeah, I guess so." I sighed. "You know, sitting here like this, with you, reminds me of how it was . . ."

"How *what* was?"

"Just . . . how it used to be at home. Before Sam died."

"Really? How so?"

"Just, you know . . . in the summer, on a day like today. Dad would grill burgers on the deck, and Sam would 'help,' which basically meant standing next to Dad and passing him the hamburger flipper whenever he needed it. Even when he was really little, Dad would pretend Sam was actually useful. Mom and I would sit nearby with a drink, and watch, and try not to laugh our sodas out our noses, because the hamburger flipper was bigger than Sam was, and he looked so silly. But he was so proud."

"It sounds nice," said Jasper. "Relaxing."

"Yeah," I said. "I guess that's what I always thought family was supposed to be. Relaxing. You know?"

"Not *quite*," said Jasper, shaking her head.

"Well, that was how it was, for me," I said. "Not perfect.

My parents are . . . parents. And Sam drove me crazy, jumping on things all the time, and telling me about his boring video games nonstop. But I mean, it's like . . . school can be hard and friends are complicated, sometimes. Mean girls pick on you and boys tease you and teachers are confusing. But at home, for me, it was always just . . . home. Dad was a dad and Mom was a mom, and Sam and I were the kids, and we did things the way we did things. We knew how to be us. So even when we fought and annoyed each other, it just felt easy. Because I always knew how things would be."

"That sounds really nice," said Jasper. "My house wasn't like that at all."

"No?" I said, turning around to face her.

"No. Just . . . no."

She didn't say anything more, so after a moment I turned back around, stared at the step below me. "Well, it was like that for me. But then Sam died. And it was like . . . we didn't know how to be *us* anymore, without him. Like we were a table that lost a leg, and now the whole thing was tilted. And I guess that's not really a table, is it? It's never relaxing or easy, anymore."

I paused and waited for Jasper to say something in reply. It felt like I'd been talking for too long. But when I turned to look at her again, Jasper was just staring at me hard, and looking sad, like she might cry. I didn't want that. I didn't want things to be sad and hard here. I hadn't meant to do this, to change the way things felt in this magical place. I wanted it to be all pickles and root beer. That was the whole point of helping.

"Anyway!" I said as cheerfully as I could. "I only really meant to say how nice this is, to sit on a porch, like I used to do at home. It's such a regular thing to do. And I haven't done it in so long. Isn't that funny?"

Jasper shook her head. She was still wearing her serious face. She took a slow sip of her drink and said, "Hey, I know I probably don't need to say this. But I'm going to anyway, just in case."

"What?" I asked.

"You can't tell anyone," she said. "About me, or this place. Nobody at all."

"Oh, I know," I said. "Anyway, I wouldn't want to. I like it like this. Just us. A secret."

Jasper nodded. "Right, okay," she said. "But it's more than that. This isn't a game. We aren't playing Narnia or Hogwarts. This is my real life. It would be bad for a lot of people if anyone found me here."

"What kind of bad?" I asked. "How bad?"

Jasper shook her head. "Don't worry, nobody would die or anything. Just—I'm supposed to be living with my sister, and she doesn't care that I left. She's got her own kids to take care of. And—other problems. But if anyone found out I wasn't at her place, and that she hadn't reported me missing, she'd get into big trouble."

I didn't know what trouble she meant, really. In fact, I had a hard time wrapping my head around it. I couldn't fathom how her sister could possibly let her run off. Or why she was living with her sister in the first place. But Jasper's voice was so serious, and I knew what she needed me to say.

"Sure." I nodded. "I get it."

"Good," said Jasper. "Thank you."

"How old is she, your sister, anyway?" I asked.

"Twenty-nine," said Jasper.

"Wow, that's old!"

"Yeah, but we have different dads," said Jasper, as though that explained everything.

"Oh," I said. "How many kids does she have?"

Jasper took a swig of her root beer. "Two. A girl and a boy. Madison and Connor. And they're cute, but, wow, are they busy. Lots of work!"

"I bet," I said.

"Anyway," said Jasper, "the point is that my sister doesn't need any more stress right now. She didn't mind me leaving. She knows I can take care of myself for a while. But I swore I wouldn't get her into any trouble. And I won't. Okay? I can't. If anyone found out, I don't even know exactly what would happen. Foster care, I guess, for me."

"Foster care?"

"Maybe. Or some kind of group home. I'm not sure."

"There's a boy in my class," I said. "Seth. And he was in

foster care, when we were littler, and then his foster parents adopted him, and they actually seem pretty great. His mom was our room parent last year, and—"

"What's your point?"

"Oh, I just . . . I don't know. I thought it might help, to know that it's not always so bad. Maybe?"

It took her a minute to reply. At first I thought she was mad at me, but when she finally spoke, her voice just sounded sort of quiet. "The truth is, I don't know what it would be like. My mom made it sound . . . not good. She called it *the System*. She said I didn't want to be in *the System*. That if that happened, I'd be really unhappy, and we'd never be back together."

"Oh," I said.

"So maybe you're right. My mom was unreliable for sure. But whatever *the System* would be like, I don't think it would be like . . . this."

I looked out at the green vines sprawling all over. There was a hummingbird just a few feet away, zipping around. "Yeah," I said. "I see what you mean."

"Thanks," Jasper said, polishing off her soda and setting the bottle down on the step below her.

I wondered again what exactly had happened to make Jasper leave her sister's house. But I didn't say anything else. She didn't want to talk anymore, and I figured we had plenty of time. All the time in the world.

We just sat there together then. Feeling sorry for each

other, I guess, and feeling sorry for ourselves, but lucky too. Feeling everything. All the things. Holding on to everything at once.

Then I looked up and realized the sky had pinked up like it does sometimes in the summer, before the sun goes down. I sighed and rose from my step. "Well," I said. "I should head home, I guess."

Jasper jumped up. "Thank you. Seriously, this place is so much better now. I really appreciate everything."

"Oh, sure," I said. "It was fun."

We stood there for a second, like neither of us was sure what to do next. I didn't want to leave, but I knew I had to. I almost wanted to hug her, but I knew that would be weird. "Hey," I said at last. "One more thing. Before I go, can I get your number?" I pulled out my phone.

Jasper shook her head. "I don't have a phone," she said. "Wish I did."

"Really?" I asked, puzzled. "I could've sworn I saw you checking a phone earlier, at the bus stop."

"Yeah," said Jasper. "But I don't have a number or any cell service. It's just an old phone of my sister's. She gave it to me so I can check in with her when I'm near free Wi-Fi. Like at a coffee shop. And I have some dumb games on it."

"Oh. So that means that when you're here, you have no way of calling or emailing or anything at all?"

"Nope," said Jasper, grinning. "I'm super-extra old school.

If I need you, I'll just have to scream real loud."

I laughed. "Well, feel free to scream any old time."

"Will do!" said Jasper. "And maybe I'll see you tomorrow?"

"Definitely," I said. "Come over!"

"I will," she said. "But also, you can come here too. Now that you know everything."

"I will too!" I called out as I scrambled down the hill and pushed my way through the vines and brambles to the creek bed. I picked my way carefully down the creek as the pink sky deepened above, and then sprinted hard once I hit the pavement.

Now that I knew everything? I didn't feel like I knew anything at all. As full as the day had been, I'd barely scratched the surface. But even so, what a day it had been. A filthy, sweaty, magical, confusing day.

Back at home, I stepped up to the front door and peered through the glass. My parents were in the living room, sitting on the sofa. Plates on the coffee table in front of them. Mom with her salad. Dad with what looked like a frozen pot pie. It was strange to see them like that. Through glass. Almost like I was watching a movie about them.

They sat together, but apart, at opposite ends of the couch, facing the TV. It was funny, how a TV let you be *with* someone even if nobody touched or said a word. I wondered if either of them was even paying attention to the show. They both looked lost in thought.

But I couldn't stand there forever like that. I had to step into the room, so I put my hand on the doorknob and turned it. Mom looked up, saw me, and clicked the remote in her hand, right away. The TV went dark.

"Leah!" she said. "How was your day? Who were you with?"

"Oh, a new friend," I said. "You don't know her. And it was fun. But I'm really stinky. I walked all over today. Red's Farm and the neighborhood. Just exploring. I think I'll go take a shower."

"Okay," she said. "That's fine. But come say hello when you're done."

"Okay."

I quickly cut through the room and toward the hallway, but then Dad called out. "Oh, hey, Leah?"

I turned back around in the doorway. "Yeah?"

"I just wondered . . . did you do some work in the yard this week? I noticed someone mowed."

"Yeah!" I said, scrambling to remember what he was talking about. It seemed like it had been weeks since I'd mowed and raked. So much had happened since then. "Yeah, that was me. A couple of days ago. I'd almost forgotten about that. It just was looking kind of ratty around here."

"Well, that's nice of you!" said Dad. He sounded more

excited than an hour of raking should really make anyone. "Thanks, kiddo."

"You're . . . welcome," I said. "It was no big deal. I was bored, and it seemed like a thing I could do. To help out."

"It was," said Mom, nodding. "It was really thoughtful."

Then we all were quiet for a minute, and I couldn't tell if there was something else I was supposed to say. I stood there, waiting, in the hallway, until the TV clicked back on and released me.

LOOKING UP

The next morning, I woke up different. Or rather, I woke up *differently*. All at once, the second my eyes fluttered open. I sat up in a rush and realized I was excited. *Excited?* I couldn't remember the last time I'd woken up excited.

It was the way I used to wake up on Saturday mornings with Sam. On the weekends, Mom and Dad liked to sleep in, and so the rule had always been that Sam and I could watch as much TV as we liked, and eat anything we wanted for breakfast, so long as we were quiet.

"Don't disturb the bears," Dad would say.

So if I woke up first, I'd knock on Sam's door, and if he woke up first, he'd come into my room and tap on my forehead. Then we'd head to the living room for cookies with canned whipped cream or ice cream sandwiches or BBQ potato chips.

Saturday mornings hadn't felt that way since last year. Sneaking into the living room alone didn't feel the same, and neither did eating junk food for breakfast. Instead, I stayed in bed and tried to force myself back to sleep. But now I found myself with that Saturday-morning feeling at the thought of heading back over to Jasper's house. So I pulled on a sundress and a pair of sandals, gave my teeth a quick scrub, and quietly made my way down the hall, past my parents' door, which was still closed, though the clock on the wall told me it was after nine. I left a note on the kitchen table:

Going to the coffee shop for a muffin. Back later.

The day was already crackling hot when I stepped through the kitchen door and into the driveway, but the sun felt good on my shoulders, coming out of the chilly air-conditioning inside. I was out in the street and walking fast when I had a thought and stopped. I turned back home, but instead of the house, I went to the garage.

We'd never really used our garage to store our cars like other people did. The garage was small for two cars, and Mom and Dad had never been able to agree on whose car got to go in it. They'd decided long ago it was better if neither one did.

"Better two cars with equal amounts of bird poop than one clean car and a divorce," Dad had said.

So the garage was mostly a spider habitat and a place to store all the junk that didn't really have a spot inside the house. Now I pushed the door open and stumbled into a decade of outgrown tricycles and broken mops and boxes of hand-me-down rain boots that had never been handed down. There was slightly broken furniture that Mom intended to drag to the curb, but apparently not until it had a half inch of dust on it. It was almost like she couldn't let things go until they'd gotten so filthy she would never let them inside the house again.

I sneezed twice as I moved partway through the mess, and then I reached up and flicked on the light. Across the room I spotted what it was what I'd come for: a blue plastic cooler, hung on the wall by its handle, beside a tangled pile of bright orange extension cords.

To get to it, I stepped over an old green end table, covered in mildewed paperback books, and then a huge clear plastic bag full of Duplo blocks. I made my way across the room, but halfway there, I found that there was a spot in the middle of the garage where it looked like someone had recently cleared away all the junk and laid down a fresh blue tarp in the empty space. I was standing in the middle of the tarp when it hit me that it wasn't dusty at all. Instead, the tarp was covered in paint drips. Fresh ones. As if someone had been working on a project and stepped away only a few hours ago. But who, and what? I looked around in every direction and didn't see what someone might have been painting. There was nothing.

At least this spot is easier to walk through, I thought, and stepped over to the wall to reach for the cooler. But when I did, I jostled the extension cord loose, and it came tumbling down from its rusty nail and rained down right on top of me. I let go of the cooler and threw my hands up over my head, but when I did, I stumbled, and we all fell together—me, the cooler, and the jumble of orange cord.

"Ouch," I said softly, sitting up on the tarp and brushing dead moths from my hair. I sneezed twice and wiped at the dust on my face with an equally dusty hand. Ugh.

I could only pray that Mom and Dad hadn't woken up to the sounds in the garage. As quietly as possible, I reached over and tried to untangle the cooler from the extension cord. But when I did that, I happened to glance up, up at the ceiling, where the one bare light bulb burned. I caught my breath when I saw what it illuminated.

A cornfield.

Stretched across the ceiling, someone had been painting a cornfield. A farm. Miles of green and gold, tiny cornstalks waving in an imaginary breeze. A vast blue sky was spread over the field, shimmering with heat and sun, broken by the occasional bird. And cutting through the field was a small brown road that ran to a white farmhouse off in the distance.

I sat there, on the tarp, staring at that field, lush and thick, with bits of light scattered everywhere. I couldn't take my eyes away from it.

Then I noticed a single brown spot, lost in the sea of green. I stood up and stretched to my tiptoes, but I couldn't quite make it out. I dragged a chair over and climbed up to peer closer. The brown spot was a head of hair, and beneath the hair was a face. It was a small boy lost in the sea of green.

I stared at that boy, drowning in his field. I stared, and closed my eyes as I felt a sob rising in my throat. Then I swallowed the sob, opened my eyes, and climbed down off the chair.

There was only one person who could have painted this field. But Dad didn't paint anymore, ever. In fact, he didn't do much of anything but sit and stare at his phone. Part of me wanted to run inside and knock on my parents' door, pull my father out of his room and the chilly house, into the hot garage, to tell me what this was on the ceiling. But I didn't. If he wanted anyone to know about this, then he wouldn't have been doing it in secret in the garage without telling us. And if he didn't want to talk to me, I wasn't going to ask him. He could keep his secret. I had my own.

I quickly returned the extension cord to the wall, put the chair back where I'd found it, and swept the dead moths and dust from the blue tarp. Then I turned off the light, closed the door behind me as quietly as I could, and ran to Jasper's, the cooler bumping against my legs. I'm not sure why, but suddenly, I was in a hurry. I felt like I was racing something, although I wasn't sure what. My sandals thwacked the street all the way there, and by the time I was cutting up along the creek, my blood was racing in my ears, and I was out of breath.

It felt good to run. Away.

When I pulled myself up the hill of kudzu and popped through into the secret green world, I saw Jasper right away, sitting on the stoop in front of the house. And my hurry disappeared. My breath slowed and the day all around me softened, relaxed. I raised the cooler and waved it at her. "Look!" I said. "I brought you a present."

She was swigging out of a root beer bottle. When she saw me, she waved back. "Hey!"

I walked over. "Root beer for breakfast?"

"No, silly!" she said. "I refilled it with water."

"Ah, okay," I said, walking up the steps and sitting down on the step beneath her. Then I added, "I brought you a cooler!"

"Perfect." She laughed. "Now we just need an ice maker."

"Yeah, well, one thing at a time."

We sat for a minute like that. Jasper was sipping her water, and I was still trying to catch my breath, but also trying to decide whether to tell her about the mural on the ceiling of the garage. It felt important—that my dad was painting something, and that he was doing it alone, in secret—but I wasn't sure exactly why or what it meant. And I knew it wouldn't sound important if I said it out loud. *My dad is painting a cornfield on the ceiling* just sounded bizarre inside my head.

Instead I asked, "So, what do you want to do today?"

Jasper set down her bottle. "Hmm. Good question. What are our options?"

"Well," I said. "I don't have any especially great ideas. We can sit around here or go wandering. My parents are at home today. Saturday. So it's probably better to stay away."

"Ahhh," said Jasper. "Well, then, *besides* hanging out with your parents, what would you do today, if you could do anything? Like, if you could make a wish?"

I thought for a minute before I said, "Orlando. I'd wish to go to Orlando."

"Really?" Jasper said. "Have you ever been to Orlando? It's not awesome."

"Hogsmeade, silly," I said. "Harry Potter world. I've never been."

"Ohhhh, that *would* be nice," Jasper said. "But I'd wish for the real thing, if we're wishing. If we could really go to Hogwarts. Either that or Paris. Or maybe I'd just go swimming."

I looked up. "Swimming?"

"Sure," said Jasper. "I haven't been swimming in a long time. I love to swim. And it's so hot, and I'm *so* sweaty and gross. I could use a bath."

I hadn't thought about the fact that Jasper didn't really have any place to shower. "But there *is* somewhere to go swimming," I said, standing up and turning around to face her. "We don't need wishes for that."

"Where?"

"Just over in Grant Park," I said.

"Where's that?" asked Jasper. "Is it far? Is it nice?"

"You haven't been to Grant Park?"

She shook her head. "I haven't been anywhere, much."

"I thought everyone knew Grant Park," I said. "It's huge. The zoo is there, and there's festivals and things all summer long. And there's a public pool, with a splash pad and everything. It's less than a mile away."

"Are you kidding me?" Jasper jumped up from her step. "I haven't been swimming in forever. Can we go? Please? Right now?"

"Sure!" I said.

"I don't have a suit," she said, "but maybe I can just wear shorts?"

"I can loan you a suit. We'll just have to swing by my house first."

"But what about your parents?" asked Jasper.

"Oh, they're okay," I said. "They drive me nuts, but they won't be rude or anything. And anyway, they'll probably still be sleeping."

Before I had even finished the sentence, Jasper was off the

step and headed down the hill. "Come on!" she cried.

I followed, smiling. Running hard again. Thinking about how easy it was to make Jasper happy. And how nice that was, for a change.

A QUICK DIP

I was wrong. My parents weren't asleep when I got home. As I opened the front door and stuck my head into the living room, I heard noises from the kitchen—coffee cups and NPR.

Behind me, Jasper whispered, "I'll just wait out here." And before I could say anything, she slipped away, down the steps.

I stepped inside, and right away, Mom was standing in front of me. "Leah! There you are," she said. "Your dad and I were just wondering when you'd be back."

"I left a note," I said.

She nodded stiffly. "Yes, we found it. But we weren't sure how early you went out. It seems like you've been coming and going a lot the last few days."

"Oh," I said. "It was . . . just a little while ago. I just came back to grab my swimsuit. I'm . . . going swimming with a friend."

Mom looked more interested than usual. "Swimming with a friend? That's a nice thing to do on a hot day. Is the pool open this early?"

"I'm not sure," I said. "But we can hang out at the park until it does."

"Okay," said Mom. "Who's the friend? Tess?"

"Oh, no," I said. "Tess isn't here this summer. This is . . . a new friend I met. But that reminds me, I saw Bev yesterday. She said to tell you hi. She was on her way to some meeting."

"Oh!" said Mom, momentarily distracted. "That's . . . nice."

"She said you should call her," I added.

Mom closed her eyes briefly, a long blink. Then she opened them again and shifted the subject back. "So this new friend of yours, she's the same girl from yesterday?"

"Yeah, she's just moved to the neighborhood and hasn't been to Grant Park before. I told her I'd show her the pool. She's waiting for me, so I'm in kind of a hurry." All these words tumbled out of my mouth, and it felt like I was saying too much, and also a little like I was lying, even though everything I was saying was true.

"We'd love to meet her. It sounds like you girls are really hitting it off."

"Sure!" I said. "But she's . . . not here right now." I

supposed this was technically true, since *here* and *out in the street* aren't exactly the same.

Mom smiled. "Well, okay, have fun. Don't forget sunscreen."

"Thanks!"

I headed for my room, where I grabbed a couple of bathing suits from my dresser. Then I searched around the closet for my goggles. I hadn't been swimming in a long time, and I couldn't remember seeing my goggles in forever, but I hated to swim without them. They weren't in there. And they weren't under my bed or in the corner under the chair either.

At last, I sighed, walked over to my desk, and pulled open my junk drawer. My dreaded junk drawer. The land of no return. It was a total disaster, but when I couldn't find something, it usually turned up in there.

Once, a few years back, Dad and Mom had had a fight about making me clean my room. Mom had been yelling at me about all the little toys and trinkets I'd strewn all over my furniture and floor. She'd told me that everything had a place, and my job was to put things in their right places. Dad had laughed at her. I remembered how he'd picked up a Popsicle stick with flowers drawn on it in glitter glue. "And where do you suppose the proper place for *this* is?" he'd asked Mom. "Give the kid a little leeway, Rachel."

Mom had stared at him for a minute and then gone over to my desk, opened the bottom drawer, pulled out my construction paper and modeling clay, and moved them to the office. From that day forward, whenever I wanted to keep little things that didn't have a place, I'd just shoved them into the drawer. I almost never opened it except to shove more in, so it was always stuffed full. But somehow it made me feel good, to know that if I wanted to save something, I could. That there was a place for the things that had no other place.

Now, as I reached to pull it open, the drawer jammed. It wouldn't open at all. Almost as if someone was inside the drawer, pulling from the other side. I yanked on it and rocked the whole desk. I could almost feel the room shaking. *Argh*. I tried to wiggle it, jimmy it loose, but nothing worked.

Finally, I gave up. Jasper was waiting, and this was taking way too long. I'd just have to deal with chlorine eyes. Swimsuits in hand, I ran to the linen closet for towels, and then I made for the living room. But just as I was opening the front door, Mom appeared in the hallway and called out after me.

"Hey, Leah, can we say you'll try to be home by four? We haven't seen you much lately. It seems like you're always either gone or sleeping. Your dad and I thought it might be nice to go out for sushi or something. Reconnect."

Reconnect? What was she talking about? We hadn't *connected* in a year. But I nodded at her. "Sure," I said as I pushed on the screen door and stepped outside. I liked sushi.

And moments later, dinner was the farthest thing from my mind as Jasper appeared from behind the azaleas, and together we ran down the street, racing for the park.

We arrived just as the pool was opening. A few old men were there already at the gate, looking very serious in their swim trunks, and probably planning to hog the pool for lap swim. Then there was a whole crew of moms with little kids waiting. A few dads too. They had huge picnic baskets and folding chairs, and I knew they'd stay all day, the parents talking to each other and the kids peeing in the splash pad and falling over and crying. Jasper and I hung back and let the crowd go ahead of us.

But at last the line was gone and it was our turn. We darted inside, pulled on our suits, took a two-second obligatory shower just inside the gate, and then ran to spread out our towels in the shadiest spot we could find, which was unfortunately close to a massive trash can.

"What a view!" said Jasper, nodding at the garbage. "With any luck we'll have flies in a few minutes. Maybe bees too!"

"I know, but I promise, by noon we'll be glad for a spot under the tree," I said. "I know what I'm talking about."

"If you say so," said Jasper.

"I do," I said, and sank down on my towel.

Suddenly, I heard someone calling my name. A grown-up voice. I turned around. "Leah Davidson!" called out Mrs. Hanson, waving as she walked our way. She was wearing a flowered swimsuit with a ruffled skirt and clutching a squirming baby in a floppy hat. The baby did not look happy about the hat.

"Hi," I said, standing up. "How are you and, umm . . . *her*?" I couldn't remember the baby's name.

"We're fine," Mrs. Hanson said. "Mostly, anyway. The baby isn't sleeping terribly well. And she has a funny rash. But that's sure to go away, I suppose."

I didn't know the first thing about rashes, so I just nodded and said, "Sure! Umm, hey, Mrs. Hanson, this is my new friend, Jasper. Jasper, this is Mrs. Hanson. She teaches first grade."

"Lovely to meet you," said Mrs. Hanson distractedly. The baby was chewing on her hat string. "Any friend of Leah's . . ."

Jasper grinned. "What was Leah like in first grade? Did she eat too much paste?"

"Oh!" said Mrs. Hanson. "I didn't have Leah in my . . . well, that is to say . . . she had another teacher. I, umm . . . I had her . . ."

"She taught Sam," I explained, as Mrs. Hanson glanced down, staring intently at the top of the hat. "She was Sam's favorite teacher of all time. Right, Mrs. Hanson?"

Mrs. Hanson nodded.

"I remember that Sam picked out that huge orange candle for you, for your birthday. He bought it with his own money, at the farmers market. He saved up."

"Yes, I remember. I still have it," said Mrs. Hanson gently, but she still wasn't making eye contact with me.

Then there was a pause, until at last Mrs. Hanson cleared her throat. "Okay, well, I think maybe Olive here should get over to her little buddies to splash. But it was nice seeing you, Leah. Please, dear, tell your mom hello from me. It's been too long." She turned to leave.

That probably would have been a good way to end things, but right then something funny happened. Inside me. A little twisting snake of a feeling. I don't know where it came from, but I was just so tired of this same dumb interaction, which I seemed to have with everyone. *Everyone* wanted me to tell my parents hello. *Everyone* had trouble making eye contact and *everyone* said those same words, *It's been too long.* Now, for some reason, I couldn't let Mrs. Hanson just walk away. Not this time.

"You know," I shouted after her, "you could call, if you want."

"What's that?" she said, looking back over her shoulder. "What do you mean, Leah?"

"I mean, you could call my mom. You could check in."

"Oh, yes, I suppose," she said, nodding sadly. "I suppose I should. It's just . . . you know, been a busy year."

"Really?" I said. "It's mostly been quiet at our house. Super quiet."

Mrs. Hanson stared at me for a second, as the baby made a

gurgling noise and then said "Ba!" in her arms.

"I mean, it's been quiet ever since the funeral. Nobody ever calls or stops by."

"Oh, Leah," said Mrs. Hanson, even though the baby was squirming now. "I'm so sorry, dear." She looked incredibly sad, but also incredibly uncomfortable.

Then things were quiet again, and Jasper coughed, which somehow made it feel okay when Mrs. Hanson turned to go. "Well, I just wanted to . . . you know, check in, Leah. And maybe . . . I'll see you soon."

I watched her walk away, out the main gate and off to the parking lot, with her baby staring back at us all big-eyed and drooly. Even though they had only just arrived. I couldn't stop staring back.

After that, Jasper and I got into the water and paddled around. Jasper swam a quick lap across the pool and back, then ducked down to do some somersaults beside me, but when she burst up out of the water, she said, "Hey, Leah!"

"What is it?" I asked.

"Why did you do that to that teacher?"

"Do what?" I swam away from her.

"*You know,*" she said, following me, treading water. "You intentionally made that woman uncomfortable. Didn't you?"

I turned and splashed at her lightly. "Kind of, I guess. I wasn't *trying* to do it. But then, yeah. I guess maybe I did know she was uncomfortable."

135

"That wasn't nice," said Jasper.

"No, I guess it wasn't," I said.

"Well, okay then," said Jasper. And she swam off to the deep end.

I wasn't exactly sure why I'd done it, and I knew I couldn't explain it to Jasper. It was just a thing I'd done, because it had been in me to do. Because there was a broken little place inside me. A crumpled piece of paper I couldn't straighten out. Because I was tired of everything being wrong with everyone I'd known all my life. Because it didn't seem fair that some people got to be busy and comfortable, and others didn't. Because saying the wrong thing felt better than keeping silent any longer.

A year was a long time to be silent.

I sank under the water and held my breath for a full minute.

THE VINE REALM

After that day, I tried not to go places where we'd see people I knew. It was better just to be with Jasper. When we were all alone together, summer felt right. Like a little island of time set apart from the rest of the year. The days drained away like they're supposed to. Like something you want to savor. Slowly, but still too fast.

Sometimes, Jasper would turn up on my porch in the morning after my parents had left for work, and together we'd make breakfast and spend a lazy morning watching TV or sitting around, talking. Normal things, like I used to do with Tess. The things I'd always done, until Sam died. One morning we gave ourselves facials. Another day, we weeded the incredibly overgrown garden my mom had been neglecting all year. I had no idea what I was doing, and I don't think Jasper really did either, but it was nice to sit in the sun and dig in the dirt and smell all the green growing things. And that evening, when my mom came home from work, she noticed right away, perked up, and said, "Well, look at that! You know, Leah, I was a little nervous about you just hanging around the house, but I have to admit, you seem really mature this summer. . . ."

I'd never really cooked for anyone but myself before, but knowing Jasper didn't have a working stove made me want to. *Mature* or not, I'd probably have grumped about it if my parents had asked me to cook dinner for them, but it didn't feel like work, not with Jasper sitting beside me on the counter, her long legs hanging down, as she sipped a cup of coffee. I felt older, somehow. I felt like a person instead of just a kid. And so we made messy omelets that gooped onto the plate. Grilled cheese and tomato sandwiches. Tater Tots. I'd tie on my dad's *Watcha Cooking, Hot Stuff?* apron that he used to wear when he grilled, and lean into the fridge, happily.

Once in a while, Jasper would ask to take a shower or to wash her laundry, but mostly, she didn't ask for things. She left it to me to offer. Which made me want to offer her everything.

On the mornings Jasper didn't come to my house, I walked over to hers. And those days were just as good. We'd pick the wild berries along the fence on Mercer, washing them with the farm's hose, or we'd walk the creek, looking for pieces of colored glass smoothed down by time and water.

One day, in the creek, I heard Jasper give a loud shout, and came running to find her waving something in the air. "Look at this guy," she said. "He's huge!" When she stopped waving her hand, I could see she was clutching a large crawfish. He wasn't moving, probably stunned by the wild ride Jasper had given him.

"I'm going to keep him for a pet," she said. "His name is Fido. I've never had a pet before."

She looked so proud of her find, I didn't tell her I knew this particular crawfish already. Sam had caught him at least three times.

"I think maybe you should let him go," I said. "He's got to be really old, to be so big, don't you think? It would be a shame if he died in your house. I bet he'd smell."

Jasper pouted at me. "I know," she said. "I was just kidding, mostly."

I stood there, watching Jasper set him back down, and thinking about how Sam used to wave the crawfish at me, even though he knew I hated it. I'd always been so angry at him when he did things like that, pranks and tricks. But it was impossible to be angry at him now.

A few times I treated Jasper to ice cream at Morelli's—always salted caramel for me, but Jasper ordered something different every time. Weird flavors, like rosewater or olive oil. Earl Grey or jalapeño coconut.

"Are you crazy?" I would always ask. "What if you don't like it?"

"But what if I do?" asked Jasper. "What if it's the best thing ever, and I don't try it, and I die, years from now, old and miserable, wondering . . ."

"It seems unlikely you'll be thinking about ice cream when you die," I said.

"You never know," said Jasper, licking her cone thoughtfully. "There are definitely worse things to be thinking about when you die. It might be my last gasp. *Earl. Grey. Tea!*" We both laughed.

One day, Jasper was over at my house, running a load of laundry, and she happened to notice the art supply cabinet in the office. She swung the door open and peered inside.

"Hey, what's all this for?" she asked as she picked up a little box of purple seed beads and shook it at me, like a maraca. She reached for a bottle of poster paint.

"Nothing really," I replied. "Dad used to do art projects with Sam and me. You know—tie-dyeing and stuff like that. But he doesn't anymore. He says he doesn't have time these days, for art."

Staring at the paint in Jasper's hand, I thought briefly about the cornfield in the garage. I'd been out to see it a few more times during the day, when I wasn't with Jasper and I knew nobody would come home. I couldn't quite tell if it had changed or not, if he was still working on it. But I liked to stand and look at it in the dusty garage light. It made me want to cry, every time, but in a way that felt right. Like stretching, almost, or yawning. I hadn't told Jasper about it, and somehow, I still didn't want to. I didn't want to share it.

"No time for art?" Jasper said. "What's he so busy with?"

I shrugged. "Working. Checking his email. Being a dad. Who knows." I turned to the wall above the desk and pointed at a still life, a painting of a fruit bowl, only there were other things in the bowl too. Keys, a broken Barbie doll head, random junk along with the apples and pears. "My dad painted that. He painted most of the pictures around the house. Once upon a time, before I was born, he wanted to be a professional artist. He even went to college for it. And when I was a kid he took me to the art museum all the time. But he doesn't talk about painting much anymore."

Jasper looked at the painting for a minute. "I like it," she said.

"Yeah, me too."

"What *does* he do for a living?" asked Jasper. "You never talk about your parents, really. I'm not even sure what their names are."

"You never talk about yours either," I said.

For weeks, we'd pretended to ignore the conversations we obviously weren't having. As wonderful and comfortable as we were with each other, there were gaps, holes, empty places in our friendship. Jasper didn't come around when my parents were home. And I never asked about her family. We both saw the gaps and knew they were there. Only now we'd stumbled into one of them.

But I didn't want things to be tense, and there was really no reason not to talk about Dad's job. So I shrugged and said, "Honestly, his job is kind of dumb. I'm not even really sure what he does. Something boring at a desk that means he needs to wear a button-down shirt. He works for a company that makes toilet paper."

"Oh," said Jasper. "Toilet paper?"

"Yeah," I said. "It's not very interesting."

She laughed. "He *seriously* switched from art to toilet paper?"

"Yeah, I guess he did," I said. "But I never thought about it like that. He never seemed to mind his job. It was just his job. Most of what he was didn't have anything to do with that. Mostly, he was a dad. "Anyway," I added, "the exact same thing happened to Mom. She was a poet a long time ago, and now she writes for the newspaper. She started doing that after I was born. Like, it made sense to try to do whatever they wanted when they were young, but then I was there, and they both thought they needed a house, and groceries, and health insurance, and that sort of stuff. So Mom packed all of her poet-hippie dresses in the back of her closet, and Dad turned into Mr. Toilet Paper."

Jasper laughed. "Mr. Toilet Paper."

I laughed too. "See, it's not all boring. That was a joke we had, when we were little. We thought he actually made the toilet paper himself. He'd bring home a roll for each of us on Friday after work each week, and be, like, 'I made these ones special for you.' And then Sam and I were allowed to throw the toilet paper at each other through the air, so we'd end up with a big tangled mess of it in the yard."

"Your dad sounds *weird*." But she was grinning, so I could tell she understood.

I nodded. "He *used* to be weird. . . ."

"But not anymore?"

I shook my head slowly, thinking it over. "I guess I hadn't thought about it like this until just now, but the truth is *that's* the thing that's changed the most. That they aren't weird anymore. They were weird until Sam died. Weird and funny. Maybe they're just too sad to be weird and funny now. Too numb."

I stood there, trying to think about whether it was true, what I was saying. Deep inside, I thought it was. It was like there was a sharp clear bell ringing, like I'd stumbled onto the truth, even if I didn't quite understand it.

Then I thought about Dad's secret. About the cornfield in the garage. The one weird thing he had left. Except that he wasn't sharing it. He was keeping it to himself. What did *that* mean?

And standing there, with Jasper and the art supplies, I suddenly had an idea. "Hey!" I said so sharply that Jasper jumped. "I know something neat we could do!"

"I'm in!" said Jasper right away, even though she had no idea what I was thinking about. "I'm a fan of neat somethings."

That afternoon, we packed up all the paints and brushes we could find in the house and took them to Jasper's place. Up the creek, through the kudzu, and around the back of the house, into the kitchen. Then we stood together, staring at the one big blank wall in the room, the one over Jasper's bed, and trying to think of what kind of mural we wanted to paint.

"We need a theme," said Jasper. "What's a good theme for a mural?"

Friendship, I thought. *Magic. Summertime.* But I didn't say them out loud. They sounded cheesy and babyish, even inside my head. "I don't know," I said. "What do you mean by a theme?"

"Or maybe not a theme," said Jasper. "That makes it sound like school. I just mean that the house needs an identity, a name, an idea, something special. Like Cair Paravel or the Burrow. What's a good name for a house? What's this house all about?"

"It's a secret portal," I said. "This house is, like, a doorway to another world, *our* little world. It's a mystery to the outside world, you know? Just ours."

"Yesssssss," said Jasper. "You're right. It's a secret door. This whole house is. You crawl through the kudzu vines and you're in a different dimension, another realm. A vine realm!"

"The Vine Realm," I repeated. "That's it. We're the Keepers of the Vine Realm! It almost sounds like it came from a book, doesn't it?"

"Totally," said Jasper. "Maybe we should write it someday. But for now . . ." She stepped back, and with a pencil, in four confident strokes, she drew a rectangle in the middle of the wall over her bed. It was a door-sized rectangle, but a small one. If it suddenly turned into a real door, and we wanted to step through, we'd have to duck our heads.

"Nice," I said.

Jasper looked back at me over her shoulder. "Right?" Her face was shiny with sweat, and she looked extra alive as she turned back around and quickly added a circle for a doorknob.

For two seconds, it almost felt like she'd cast a spell, like if she wanted to, she could actually turn the knob and step through the wall. I knew it wasn't true, but it *felt* true.

"Okay," said Jasper. "Now we have our plan. Let's paint. You want to start on the door, and I'll try to figure out the vines?"

"Sure!" I said, kneeling down to open the brown paint. And then we didn't talk anymore for a while, just painted in the hot kitchen. Mosquitoes buzzed around us, and at one point the paint sloshed on the floor and we had to clean it up as best we could. But we didn't say a word. We didn't have to. It was perfect. A perfect afternoon. If we dripped now and then, it didn't matter. If the painting turned out horribly, who cared? Nobody else would ever see it. Nobody else mattered at all. That was the beauty of the Vine Realm, where we were the only people who existed in the whole entire world. Just us, the hot still summer air, the heavy smell of roses, and the occasional dill pickle. All of the sad things were outside. All of the people who had disappeared. All of the things they weren't saying to me. All of the hard, sharp memories, far away. We were making something new, all our own.

That night at dinner, over fish and peas and potatoes—which is possibly the most boring dinner in the world—my mom looked at me across the table, and asked, "What's that on your neck, Leah? It looks very . . . green?"

My hand went to my neck, and I rubbed at the mark. Sure enough, I had a big smear of dried paint I hadn't noticed. I'd been so careful to bring the leftover paint home and put it back where it belonged, with all the other art supplies, and I'd scrubbed my hands carefully, but I hadn't thought to look at my neck.

"Oh, I was just . . . painting," I said. Then I scooped up some peas and shoved them into my mouth. To give myself a chance to think of a good story. Only I couldn't think of one.

"Painting what?" Dad looked up and set down his phone.

I swallowed the peas, and when I opened my mouth, somehow the truth slipped out. "A mural," I said, and then shoveled in a too-big bite of mashed potatoes. They were the kind that came from a plastic microwave carton and tasted like it, like salt and Saran wrap. I could barely swallow the awful bite, but I kept my eyes on Dad. I watched him carefully.

"A mural, huh? That's interesting. . . ."

He was staring at me, so I stared right back. I waited, to see if he'd say any more. But he didn't. We both just sat there, and I found myself wishing, intensely, that he'd tell me right then about the mural in the garage. About the cornfield and the boy. Did Mom know about it? We were both totally silent, eating our gross potatoes. It's funny how you can be *not lying* and also *not telling the truth* in the very same moment.

Mom was oblivious. "Now, that's a fun thing to do! How creative."

"Yeah," I said, "I saw another one, that someone *else* had painted, and it gave me the idea."

"Great," said my dad, wiping his mouth with his napkin. "That sounds great."

"Where is it?" said Mom. "Your mural?"

I glugged down a sip of fizzy water as I scrambled mentally to think of the next thing I should say. "Oh, it's just at my friend's house. On her bedroom wall."

"What friend?" asked Mom.

This was the most interest they'd shown in anything I'd

done for as long as I could remember. Though, to be fair, it was also the first interesting thing I'd done that they knew about in the same amount of time. I guessed there wasn't much to ask me about lounging in my leggings and watching TV.

I prepared to lie. "Oh, just . . ."

Then I looked at Mom and Dad. They were both staring at me. And listening—really listening. For a moment, it made me want to cry, seeing how much they wanted to hear about my day of mural painting with some imaginary friend whose name I was about to make up.

Then it happened. I opened my mouth, and out came the truth again. "Her name is Jasper. I think I told you about her before, that day we went swimming?"

Mom nodded. "Oh, yes, but I guess I didn't catch her name. I'd have remembered that. *Jasper*. How unusual, for a girl."

"Yeah, well, I met her at the farm, taking a walk. She's just moved to the neighborhood. She's really nice. We've been hanging out."

I sat back, instantly regretting my words. What had I done? Talking about Jasper with my parents was like telling grown-ups about Narnia. It felt like Jasper would disappear now, like I'd betrayed her and ruined everything. The secret was over. It felt like the Vine Realm might suddenly fade. Like I'd go back tomorrow and find no hole in the kudzu, no house there at all.

But amazingly, Mom just smiled. "I'm so glad you have a new friend," she said, picking up her dish and taking it to the sink. "I know you get bored when Tess isn't around."

Dad followed her lead and stood up too. "Well," he said. "That was delicious, but it's dart night, so I need to get moving."

"Okeydokey," called Mom in a false cheery voice. "Have fun!"

"Will do," said Dad, and he turned to go.

But as he left the room, keys jangling, Dad gave me a long, careful stare, as though he was thinking about something, hard. It made me wonder. About how often my dad really played darts.

And sure enough, when I peeked outside, an hour later, I saw a very faint crack of light coming from under the garage door. The thinnest sliver, as if someone had shoved a blanket under the door, hoping they could hide from sight completely. If I hadn't known to look for it, I might not have noticed at all.

That night in bed, I couldn't sleep, or even lie still. I was all tangled up in thoughts and bedsheets. I thought about my father's dart nights that he wasn't going to, and the cornfield on the ceiling. I thought about my mom sitting in the living room with her glass of wine, alone and clueless. Then for some reason, I thought about Sam, throwing toilet paper into the air.

That thought made me want to curl up in a ball, so I pushed it away and tried to imagine what Jasper was doing, alone in the Vine Realm, soothed by the twinkle lights on the floor and the mural on the wall above her. I tried to imagine what it felt like to go to sleep in a house alone, without parents to tell you anything or expect anything from you. If you didn't have to pretend you were a family when you didn't feel like a family. If you didn't have to constantly try to figure out what to say to the people who knew you best.

I knew Jasper's situation would freak my parents out, that they'd be upset if they found out I'd spent my summer in an abandoned house. In some part of my brain, I knew there were words for what was happening to Jasper. *Runaway. Homeless.* But the more time I spent with her, the less crazy it seemed that she could take care of herself. Jasper was so wise, so smart. She seemed to know everything there was to know. She seemed to have things under control.

In five years, I'd be going away to college myself. That wasn't very long. In five years, I'd be living alone too. In a room of my own, where I could paint on the wall and eat all the pickles in bed and stay up as late as I wanted, with no rules. Just like Jasper. Was this really so different from that? Five years wasn't so much.

I turned over and closed my eyes, tried to imagine I was with her, there, in the Vine Realm. She was probably still awake. Sitting on the top step of her stoop, staring up at the stars. While I was tucked neatly into my bed. I pictured the splintered wood and the tall grasses swaying in the breeze. I closed my eyes and settled into my pillow. When I took a deep breath, I could almost smell the roses.

FLAMING BRAINS

"What's it like at night?" I asked Jasper the next day. We were walking her trash to the dumpster down the street, behind the church on Woodland. The day was overcast and cooler than usual. It felt like rain, but so far, no drops.

Jasper shrugged. "At night I'm asleep. I go to bed early, because it's so dark in the house. And then I usually wake up early too."

"Like camping?"

"I guess so," said Jasper. "I've never been camping before."

"Seriously?" We stopped to throw the lid of the dumpster open, and a wave of cooking summer trash rot enveloped us. We both wrinkled our noses.

"Yep," said Jasper. "Have you been camping a lot?"

"Not a lot," I said. "And not lately. But we used to do it. Sam was in Cub Scouts, and we'd go on these big family trips with the pack. My dad used to joke that Sam was the only Jewish Boy Scout in America. It's like a thing . . . that Jews don't camp, I guess. A joke people make. I'm not sure why. Maybe because we lived in tents in the desert for forty years or something."

"Is it fun?" asked Jasper. "Camping, I mean."

"It's nice to be somewhere different," I said. "It's like you're outside your regular life. The rules are different. It's nice to wake up outside. You don't take showers. And Mom always used to let us have Froot Loops."

"What's so great about Froot Loops?" asked Jasper.

I shook my head. "It wasn't really *about* the cereal. More that Froot Loops were a thing Sam and I weren't allowed to eat at home. The point was that all the rules broke down in the woods. Food was different. Bedtime was different. My parents were different too. They would lock their phones in the car and forget they existed. My dad would play guitar by the fire, sing these cheesy songs—and, wow, is he a bad singer—but it was nice. Nobody cared. Sometimes, my mom would sit in his lap. I never saw her do that at home, ever. Outside life is . . . outside. Outside everything, I mean."

"So," said Jasper, "basically, when your family goes

camping, you all turn into wood elves?"

I laughed. "Yeah, pretty much. My mom's hair used to be super long, like I picture an elf having. Now it's short, like pixie short. She walked into a Great Clips and cut it off the morning of Sam's funeral. But before, it was the kind of hair you notice on the street. She could sit on it."

"Whoa!" said Jasper. "She really was a hippie poet, huh?"

I shook my head. "Not since I can remember, really. She mostly looked like other moms, just with super long hair. But whenever we went camping, she would do this thing, where she'd put it in two long braids. And then when we went on a hike, I'd collect things, and we'd stick them into her hair."

"Like twigs and rocks, you mean?" Jasper made a face. "Squirrels?"

"No, silly! Like flowers and leaves," I said. "Beautiful things. She'd let me weave it all into her braids. So the longer we hiked, the more she'd turn into this amazing elf queen. I loved it, seeing her like that. Once, I found a locust shell, and I touched it to her braid, just a little bit, and it clung there, like that. Holding on to her. She was so happy, she kept it there all day."

I stopped walking for a minute. That memory seemed so very far away now, so impossible. I tried to imagine what Mom would do if I tried that today, if I held up a locust husk to her. I was pretty sure she'd flinch.

"Anyway"—I took a breath—"when I tried to take the locust shell out later, it shattered, just broke right apart, in my fingers."

"Ugh," said Jasper.

But it wasn't *ugh* to me, that memory. It was beautiful. "It was so easy to pick it up and put it there, that husk, but there was no way to take it out without breaking it." I sat and thought about that for a minute.

"Ugh," said Jasper again. "So then she had dead locust bits in her hair? I think the Vine Realm is *plenty* of outside for me. You can keep your snakes and bugs and locust shells."

"Yeah," I said, shaking my head. "But the thing is, somehow bugs are different when you're camping. You just have to believe me about that. And s'mores are delicious, and flaming brains are fun."

"Well, we don't need to sleep outside to eat marshmallows," said Jasper. "What's a flaming brain?"

"It's when you set newspapers on fire," I said.

"Where I'm from that's called pyromania," said Jasper.

"No," I said, laughing. "It's not like that. You fold them up in a special way and they float. Up into the air, which is all dark and everything. They fly. Like magic lanterns."

She rolled her eyes. "Whatever you say, pyromaniac!"

"It's hard to explain it," I said, "but I could show you, if you want. What if—what if I came over after my parents go to sleep tonight? I'll bring the stuff we need, and we can make a fire."

Jasper raised an eyebrow at me. "How about we *don't* set a fire at the abandoned house where I'm sleeping."

"What if we don't do it *at* the house?" I said. "What if we go over to the farm? There's a fire pit there. Totally safe." I couldn't believe what I was suggesting. I'd never even thought about sneaking out before. But it was exciting, having something I knew about and Jasper didn't.

"Sure," said Jasper with a shrug. "It's not like I've got other plans."

That afternoon, before Mom and Dad came home, I assembled my supplies. We didn't have all the stuff for s'mores, but I found a bag of marshmallows and a stack of newspaper. I grabbed a thick old quilt to sit on, and a big box of matches. Then I rummaged in the closet under the stairs until I found the camping lantern. But just as I was fitting everything into a mesh beach bag, I heard a clap of thunder.

I ran to the window as the storm swept in. The sky was suddenly dark as dusk, and rain spattered the porch. Not a crazy summer storm that might be over soon. The kind of heavy, steady rain that goes on for days sometimes. Soaks everything, ruins entire weekends.

"Perfect," I said out loud. "Just perfect." There was no

way we could start a fire in the storm, and I'd be soaked by the time I got to Jasper's if I tried to walk.

That's when Mom's car pulled into the drive, and I had to scurry to my room, to stash my supplies in the closet.

It rained all through dinner. It rained as I loaded the dishwasher. It rained as Mom and Dad silently watched some boring documentary on the TV, and I hid in my room, trying to decide whether to sneak out after all. It would definitely be better to wait until another night, but now Jasper was expecting me, and I didn't want to let her down.

Then, just as Mom and Dad were doing their nightly routine of locking the doors and turning out the lights in the house, the rain suddenly stopped. At first I thought it was my imagination, but when I raised the window above my bed to check, all that met my face was cool night air.

"Good night!" I sang out more cheerfully than usual, as Mom walked past my door.

"Leah!" said Mom. Like she was remembering me. She stopped for a minute in the doorway, turned to look at me, standing there beside my bed.

Then she did a funny thing. She stepped into my room and walked across to me. She reached out a hand and set it on my forehead. It had been years since she'd come into my room at bedtime, really. But now she stood there, looking at me.

I realized we were almost exactly the same height. Her eyes were looking into my eyes.

"Oh, my girl," she said in a soft voice. Her hand fell away. "Time for bed." She leaned over, pulled back the covers, and motioned for me to climb in.

And it was like the little-girl part of me woke up and remembered what to do, like I was on automatic pilot. I crawled into bed and closed my eyes. I felt the cool sheet cover me.

"Mom?" I said as I turned over onto my side. "I'm not a little kid."

She smiled. "I get that." She patted my head and leaned down to kiss me at the hairline. "I just . . . wanted to."

"Okay," I said.

She walked to the doorway, but then she turned around again. "Hey," she said. "Do you remember how sometimes I used to tell you a story at night?"

"Sure," I said.

"And do you remember that sometimes I would have trouble finishing the story, and so you'd take over and finish it for me?"

I nodded.

"Do you remember any of those stories?"

I shook my head slowly. "I don't . . . think so," I said.

"Yeah, me either," she said. "But I know they were some of my favorites. I wish I could remember them now." Then she reached up and turned off the light. "Good night, Leah. Try to get to sleep."

For the first time all day, I felt guilty about sneaking out. How had she done that? It was like she'd sensed I was going to do something bad and came in to show me she was thinking about me. Like some weird mom superpower had kicked in. A guilt-inducing bedtime tuck-in mind trick.

But Jasper was waiting, and I wasn't going to let her down.

I set my alarm for midnight and plugged in my earbuds. When the chime went off, I woke up straight away, but I lay there for a while, just to be sure the house was quiet. Then I got busy, stuffing my bed with piles of dirty clothes, and stepped back to survey my work. It didn't look like me at all. It looked like a bed stuffed with dirty clothes. Still, it was better than nothing.

I grabbed my beach bag from the closet, and as quietly as I could, I crept out of the house, closing the front door so slowly behind me that it didn't make a sound.

Out in the street, I ran. The night was damp and dark, and more silent than normal. I'd never been alone at night like this, and I was a little scared. On Woodland, there were streetlights that cast an odd yellow glow and threw shadows everywhere, but once I was on the gravel road to the farm, the lights disappeared.

The rain had gone, but the sky was still overcast, and the

moon barely showed at all behind the clouds. I was lucky I knew the way so well. I didn't stumble once, though my heart was pounding.

When I got to Jasper's door, I rapped lightly and then tried the knob, but it wouldn't open. So I knocked harder, and almost immediately, Jasper's face popped into view, behind the makeshift curtain she'd fashioned out of a towel. She looked excited.

"Hang on!" she said, and I heard a funny rasping, dragging sound before the door opened to let me into the twinkle-light fairyland of the Vine Realm at night.

"What was all that?" I asked, stepping into the kitchen. "That awful noise?"

Jasper motioned to two big cinder blocks and a piece of wood. "It's not perfect," she said. "But the door doesn't lock, and so I rigged this up. Just in case someone tries to come in at night when I'm sleeping."

"Like who?" I asked, setting down my bag.

"Anyone," said Jasper. "There's literally *nobody* I want surprising me in the night."

"Right, but who would *want* to come in?" I asked. "Who would be here at night? Or in the day? Nobody even knows about this place. I've lived here all my life, and I didn't know about it."

"Oh, I don't know," said Jasper. "The police, looking for

runaways. Or some scary dude hiding from the police."

"Wow," I said. "I guess I hadn't thought about any of that."

"There's a lot of people who sleep outside," said Jasper. "I can't be the only one who knows about this place. I'm sure other homeless people would love my setup. I mean, look at it!"

"Yeah," I said, thinking about all the homeless people who shuffled around the hipster shops and bars in East Atlanta on the weekends, asking for spare change. I thought about the tired-looking men who stood by the on-ramp to the interstate with their signs that read Will Work for Food God Bless. "I guess you're right. I just hadn't thought about you that way."

"Well, *that way* is what I am," said Jasper.

"Kind of," I said. "But not really. I mean, you have a sister."

"Don't you think most homeless people have a sister?" asked Jasper. "Or a brother or a mother or a father or a kid?"

"I guess they do," I said, trying to wrap my brain around it. Though the thought was a terrible one. I decided to change the subject. "I'm not sure the fire will work. It's not raining anymore, but it's still super wet outside."

Jasper laughed and pointed to a few buckets and cans in the middle of the room, collecting drips from leaks in the ceiling. "Yeah, it's pretty wet in here too."

"Ugh," I said. "That's no fun. But anyway, I brought the other stuff we need. For flaming brains. And I found some marshmallows too."

"What are we waiting for?" Jasper slipped on her flip-flops and I hoisted the bag up on my shoulder. Then we left the house to hike back down through the kudzu, slipping a little in the mud. We walked the short trek up the creek, and then to the farm, heading for the very middle, where no tree branches would block the sky. There I unpacked my bag and laid the quilt down. Luckily it was thick enough that the wet grass didn't soak all the way through. I set out the marshmallows and the lantern in the middle of it. Then we sat down around the lantern. Almost like it was a campfire. Jasper's face glowed in the lantern light.

Once we were finally sitting down, the night changed. It settled. It calmed along with us. The sky above us was overcast, soft and thick with clouds. It looked like gray felt. All around us, the trees dripped, and each time the wind blew, a scatter of drops could be heard hitting the ground. The occasional intrepid firefly blinked here and there. Everything felt hushed and cooler than usual. Like the night was waiting.

Jasper tore open the marshmallow bag and popped one into her mouth. "Okay," she said. "What's the big deal with these brains?"

"You'll see," I said, reaching for a piece of newspaper.

I laid it out in front of me on the quilt and folded the corners like my dad had taught me, into triangles, and then I popped the whole thing open, like a sort of box.

"Is it basically a paper airplane?" asked Jasper.

"More like a blimp," I said, reaching for another piece of newspaper. I folded a second box. Then I stood and motioned for Jasper to do the same. "Come on," I said. "Not on the blanket."

We walked about twenty feet away and stood, holding our newspaper contraptions. I struck a match, watched it flare, and then lit Jasper's brain. "Okay, now let go!" I said.

As the flaming box of paper floated up into the sky, I lit my own brain and released it too. Then we both stood and watched the sky, watched the orange burning creations melt into the soft darkness above. They lifted and drifted, beyond the oak trees, and bits of ash fell down onto our heads. It was so dark I couldn't see the ash falling on my arms, but I could feel it. Like gentle whispers on my skin.

"Wow," said Jasper, once the fire in the sky was gone.

"I know, right?"

"Can we do it again?"

"Sure," I said. "Of course."

We made another set and watched them float. Then we made ten all at once, and set them all on fire as quickly as we could. They illuminated the wet branches as they rose, filled the sky with their soft, glowing embers. It was maybe the prettiest thing I'd ever seen. It was so perfect that after that, neither of us even suggested making more.

Back on the blanket, we lay on opposite sides of the camping lantern, staring silently at each other through the bright plastic glow, so different from actual fire.

"Why are they called flaming brains?" asked Jasper after a minute. She rolled over onto an elbow and reached for a marshmallow. "They don't look like brains."

"I don't know," I said. "My dad just always calls them that. We used to do them with all the neighbors, after cookouts."

"Like on the Fourth of July?"

"Yeah, but we used to have cookouts all the time," I said. "There used to be this whole crew of families that hung out together. Once a month, at least, we'd all get together at someone's house. Me and Sam and our friends would be all crazy in the yard, playing games and whacking things with sticks and running around with hot dogs and watermelon. I don't think any of us ever used a plate. And meanwhile the parents would sit on the porch and drink beers. Lots of beers."

"I know about moms and beers," said Jasper. "Does that bother you? Does your mom ever get mean?"

I shook my head. "No way, my mom only ever got really happy. Annoyingly happy. She'd drink her beer, and then laugh super loud. Like a bird, kind of, HEE-HEE."

"Yeah, that does sound a little annoying."

"It was," I said. "But it was, like, she was so, so, so happy. It kind of made me happy too. Sometimes, she'd just dance.

By herself, in the yard. She'd come down to where the kids were and dance alone, all happy. And barefoot! My mom is always taking off her shoes. Even now. But she doesn't dance anymore, or laugh like that. No more HEE-HEE. That was all before . . ."

"Before Sam?" asked Jasper.

"Yes, before Sam," I said. Then I sat up and looked at Jasper. "I wonder if the neighbors still get together, once a month, but nobody calls us anymore."

"That would be really unfair," said Jasper. "But sometimes things *are* unfair."

"Yeah. Yeah, they are. . . ."

I lay there for a minute and thought about that—about unfairness. And Sam. After a minute I said "Hey, Jasper? I think I'm ready."

"For what?" said Jasper.

"To tell you about Sam. I think I want to tell you about it. About him. What happened. I haven't told anybody. Not even my parents. I mean, they know what happened, but they don't know the whole story. What I was thinking when . . . But I want to tell *you*. If you don't mind. If you want to hear it?"

She swallowed. "Are you sure you want to tell it?" she asked.

Suddenly I *was* sure. Suddenly, it was like some aching hole was in me, like the damp dark night or the fires in the sky had changed everything. I wanted to tell Jasper what had happened. In fact, I didn't think I could stop myself.

"Yes."

"Okay," she said in a whisper that told me she was ready. Or was trying to be. So I lay back down again on the other side of the lantern. I faced Jasper, took a deep breath.

"We were at camp," I said. "It was the very last week of camp."

THE WHOLE STORY

"We both started going to camp when we were eight," I said. "Me first, and then Sam. It was a family tradition. My mom had gone to Camp Whippoorwill too, when she was eight, and her mom before her. So it was the fourth year for me, and only Sam's second year."

"What's it like?" asked Jasper. "Camp, I mean."

"Camp Whippoorwill is . . . good. Or it was for me, anyway. It was like I got to go there each year, for a whole month, and I wasn't the regular version of Leah Davidson anymore. Like my camp friends knew this other version of me. Camp Leah was louder and more fun and she laughed more. Camp Leah would do things that Regular Leah wouldn't, like water ski. I don't know why. Camp Leah wore her hair in pigtails."

"You'd look cute in pigtails," said Jasper.

"Every year, I'd promise myself that when I got back home, I'd try to keep being Camp Leah. But it never worked. I'd walk into school that first day and turn back into Regular Leah. I'd put my hair in pigtails but then take them out again. And just be my usual self, trailing after Tess and trying not to be left out of things."

"I think I get it," said Jasper.

"I know you do," I said, staring at her in the greenish light of the lantern. "Anyway, it was Sam's second year. And he was . . . well, he was my little brother. He was annoying. He didn't like it there as much as I did. And mostly, we got divided into groups at camp. So he was in a cabin for boys his age, pretty far away. But sometimes I'd see him, at the lake or the cafeteria, and he always seemed to be alone. I felt bad . . . but not bad enough to pay too much attention."

"Was he a loner at home?"

"No. He was exactly the opposite. Sam had a whole little gang of kids he loved to play with, all these boys his age in the neighborhood. But at camp it was flipped. I had my camp friends—Hazel and Tali and Jess—and he didn't seem to have anyone."

"Poor kid," said Jasper.

"Yeah, so I'd look over at lunch or dinner and see him eating quietly. He was never quiet at home. Regular Sam was fast and loud and always making crazy noises and always in a hurry or jumping on people. So much that it was embarrassing! But Camp Sam was quiet and alone. The whole time."

"That sucks," said Jasper.

"So one day, the last week of camp, I'm at the lake, with Hazel and Tali. We're out on the raft, just talking. And I look out. I see him, heading our way. Sort of a cross between a dog paddle and a crawl. He wasn't a great swimmer."

I stopped talking for a minute and saw that Jasper was staring at me now, silent. I could see it register, what I was about to tell her. She knew before I said another word. Of course she did. Just like the moment she opened the door to his room. Jasper had a weird kind of magical intuition.

"Oh, God," she said.

I closed my eyes for a minute. Then I opened them again, and she was still staring at me. I thought maybe she'd tell me to stop, but she didn't. She sat there. She was ready. And I needed her to be ready. I needed her not to freak out.

"So anyway," I said. "Anyway . . ." I took another breath. I closed my eyes, and kept them closed as I said, "It only took a minute. I saw him, swimming our way. And I was annoyed, kind of. Not in a serious way. Just, like . . . my little brother was coming to hang out with me and my friends on the raft. Which meant we were going to have to stop talking about whatever it was we were talking about. Which I don't even remember now, because it didn't matter at all. But I was annoyed."

"Yeah," said Jasper in a soft voice.

"So when I saw him, I . . . I turned away for a minute. I looked away. I think I was hoping he'd see me turning away and get the message, go find someone else to pester."

"Oh, Leah. . . ."

"Right? I'm the worst. The worst sister ever."

I opened my eyes again and looked at Jasper. I didn't know what to expect. Shock? Disgust? But she was just waiting, listening, and I wasn't sure what her face was saying, but it didn't say that I was the worst. I kept talking.

"Anyway, after a minute, when he didn't turn up at the raft, I figured he'd swum somewhere else. But when I looked around the lake for him, to see where he'd headed . . . I couldn't find him. He just . . . wasn't there. He wasn't anywhere. There was nobody swimming near the raft, or near where he'd been. The water was empty. Flat."

"So you didn't see him . . . *go?*"

I shook my head. "I didn't see anything *happen*. Because I wasn't watching. On purpose. Because I was choosing *not* to watch. I was ignoring him. When he was dying, I was ignoring him, Jasper."

"But he didn't thrash or anything? Shout? Weren't there other people around?"

"That's the thing. Nobody saw anything. He just . . . I guess he just got tired. And slipped down. He sank. Just like that."

"Just like that," whispered Jasper.

"Yeah . . . ," I said. "Just like that."

Telling Jasper was so strange. Telling anyone was so strange. I wasn't crying. Why wasn't I crying? Shouldn't I be crying? How was I able to just tell the story? Like it was any other story? Like it was something that had happened to someone else? Finally, I was saying it out loud, and I felt . . . nothing. It was like I was made of stone. It felt like the earth should rip open, like some monster should come devour me; but I just sat there, under that foggy wet sky, and said it. Like any other words. Like no big deal. I really was the worst sister ever.

"And that was all?" Jasper asked.

I nodded. "At first it was. For, like, a second. And then I freaked, jumped up. I remember my heart was beating super fast. I looked all around. Everywhere. I was turning circles on the raft, trying to look everywhere at once. It seemed crazy. I remember I worried I was overreacting. Like Tali and Hazel might laugh at me for going nuts and stressing out. But I *knew*. I just knew. He was my brother. I knew Sam, and I could feel it, that he was gone. I could feel him not being there. The hole he'd left. Already. Do you know what I'm talking about?"

Jasper shook her head. "I don't," she said. "My sister and I . . . aren't like that. But I can imagine."

"So then, there I was, looking all around me, all around the lake, at other groups of kids, trying to find his hair—he had really dark hair, like mine. Almost black. I was looking for it, and not seeing it, and it was like something was winding up inside me, as I looked, and then the winding-up thing snapped and I just started screaming and screaming. And Tali and Hazel didn't understand, because of course they hadn't even noticed him. Because he wasn't *their* brother. He wasn't theirs. He was only mine."

At last, there were tears in my eyes, waiting, trembling, and I could feel the heaving building in my chest and I knew I only had a minute before the heaving turned to crying. I could feel it coming. Like a wave about to break.

"He was mine, Jasper," I whispered. "My person. Until he wasn't anymore. And he drove me crazy, because he was always there. But then . . . he wasn't there . . . anymore. He just disappeared. When I . . ." My words disappeared suddenly. "When I . . ."

"Leah?"

"When I . . . turned away."

Then I burst. I broke. All through me it came now, like the storm earlier that night. Crashing and throbbing. I curled up into a ball and cried. I couldn't help it. Right there on the old blanket. I buried my face in the thick dusty-smelling cloth, and I cried. I cried. I cried. Alone.

I don't know how long I was like that. I cried, and Jasper let me. She didn't say anything. She just let me cry.

But then I felt her. Not a hand or a pat or a voice, but her

172

whole body, pressed against me, curling around me like Mom used to do when I was littler and I had a nightmare and crawled up into bed with her. Jasper's chin was on my shoulder, and her knees were up inside my knees. She was *there*, fitted into me. Her arm crept around me, and she held me, calming the storm. "Shhhh," she said. "Shhhh. It's okay."

It wasn't. It wasn't okay and it never would be. But it was still nice to be held. It was better than being alone. Slowly, the sobbing softened. It quieted. Until I was still. But when it was over, Jasper was still there, holding me. The two of us, lying side by side, in the fake light from the lantern. And it wasn't weird. She was just helping, holding me together. She was just taking care of me. Being there.

"So, yeah," I said at last. In a tiny voice that didn't sound like mine. "That was how it happened. That was how he died."

"And then you came home?" asked Jasper, into my hair, right behind my ear.

I flipped myself over. Our faces were close, but we weren't touching anymore. I nodded. "Yes. My parents drove up right away. A few hours later, they were there. And I remember we hugged, but they weren't real hugs. You know what I mean?"

Jasper nodded. "I do. I know exactly."

"They were numb hugs," I said. "Hugs made of . . . I don't know . . . sadness and glass. Like we were all afraid to break each other. And they were dragging the lake by then, and while

I was in my cabin, packing, they found him. His . . . body. It wasn't *him* anymore, not really. And so, yeah, we came home. And buried him."

"Just like that?" asked Jasper.

"It's a Jewish thing," I said. "You're supposed to bury people right away, get them into the ground quick."

"How quick?"

"Too quick. Or that was how it felt. To me."

"I didn't know that," said Jasper.

"Yeah, and then all these people came over to our house and brought food. So much food. When you're Jewish and someone dies, everyone comes to visit for a few days, and you have to be polite. My grandparents were here a bunch, and the neighbors and people from school. But then they all went away again and we were left behind in this house that felt the same, only not the same. And nobody thought to eat, or clean out the fridge, and the food went bad. Because nobody thought to throw anything away. So then the house smelled like death. Literally. Like rotting things."

"That's . . . awful," said Jasper. "I didn't know that either."

I nodded at her. "It's the most awful thing. To be so . . . empty. And the whole house was just gross. And it was summer, so there was no school, and eventually my parents went back to work. So there I was in this house completely full of rotting food, alone. One day I went into the kitchen and threw everything away. Every single thing in the fridge. The ketchup and the olives and the old box of baking soda that's been there my entire life. Even the ice trays. I dumped it all in the trash outside."

"Oh, Leah."

"That was when they made an appointment for me with a therapist. After I threw away the ice trays. Like it was some cry for help or something, cleaning out the fridge. But you know what? I don't think it was. It was just gross, and Mom and Dad were being depressed and lazy, and not talking at all, about anything. They had turned into ghosts, and ghosts don't clean out refrigerators. Someone had to do it. I'd do it again."

"I would too," said Jasper, nodding. "I'd do the exact same thing."

"I know you would," I said.

Then Jasper leaned in, crossed the few inches between us. She leaned in and set her forehead against my forehead. Hairline to hairline. We stayed like that, for a minute.

"Thank you for telling me. I'm glad I know."

"Me too," I said, smiling a little, and sniffing. "I kind of can't believe it."

"You can't believe that you told me?" asked Jasper.

"Yeah," I said. "That. But also that I waited so long. It's been a year. Almost a year. I've been waiting a long time to say it out loud. I think . . . maybe . . ."

"Maybe what?"

"I think maybe I thought it would make it real, to say it

out loud. Make it true. Like if nobody else ever knew how it happened, knew the things I was thinking and feeling, it was like it didn't really happen."

"Yeah," said Jasper.

"But the thing is," I said, "it *did* happen the way I remember it, and I *did* look away, and nothing can ever make that untrue. So actually, I was keeping it all to myself. Like all the badness was just for me, inside me."

Jasper nodded slowly, like she was thinking about what I'd just said. Like she was thinking about it hard. Then, suddenly, she sat straight up on the blanket and took a deep breath. She looked down at me, and I saw that there were tears in *her* eyes too. "You know, Leah," she said, "it is *not* your fault."

"I'm not sure I *do* know that," I said. "But—"

"No," said Jasper, shaking her head. "You're *wrong* about this. You're a kid and you didn't do anything wrong. It is not your fault Sam died, and I know that for sure. For *sure*. I promise you."

"Okay . . . ," I said, sitting up too, and hugging my knees. Wanting to believe she was right.

"But also, I think that maybe it's time I tell *you* a story. Okay?"

"Okay," I said again. "I'm listening."

Then Jasper took *her* deep breath, and opened *her* mouth, but at that very moment, I noticed something. I noticed that the sky wasn't so dark anymore. There was pale gray light now, behind the trees. Thin, winking light, forcing its way through the fog and the leftover rain clouds.

"Oh, no, NO!" I said, pointing at the sky behind her. "Look!"

"What?" she asked. She turned.

"Jasper," I said. "It's morning!"

FAR FROM FINISHED

I ran hard without stopping, and I was breathless when I reached my front yard. Panting as I tiptoed those last few feet up the porch steps. Maybe I could somehow sneak back in without being spotted. *Maybe they'll be in the shower*, I thought. *Maybe they'll be running late*.

No such luck. I could see them through the front window as I approached the door. They were sitting on the couch, side by side. Both of them staring straight at me as I reached for the doorknob.

I let myself in, my chest heaving, my face hot. I stood in the doorway. "Good . . . morning?"

Dad was already dressed for the day. His hair was wet, and I could see the tooth marks from his comb. Mom was in her robe. Her hair was tangled and crazy. She looked like she had the flu.

"Have a seat, Leah," Dad said, like he was in some work meeting. He pointed to a chair.

I heard him, and I tried to move forward. I willed my feet to walk, but they wouldn't obey. It was like I was frozen in the doorway, trying to catch my breath.

"Sit *down*."

This time, I did. I unstuck my feet and stepped forward, took a seat in a chair across from them. Then, as my breathing returned to normal, Dad yelled and yelled. Mom just sat there, with her hand over her mouth. Like she was trying not to yawn, or trying not to cry. Maybe both. I don't know. But Dad was on fire. It was like he hadn't talked to me in a year, and now he wanted to use up all the words. He went on and on. All about how our relationship depended on trust, and I had broken that trust, and he wasn't sure what it would take to earn it back, and if they couldn't trust me, everyone's life would become much less fun.

Fun? I thought. *Is that what this has been?* But I didn't say it.

After a little while, Dad's face was all red and Mom put a hand on his arm, and she took a turn. Like they were wrestlers, and she was tapping in now. She talked about how they weren't mad at me—well, they were, but they were mostly just worried. She talked about how they were just trying to keep me safe. About how this was a scary age, thirteen.

"Lots of kids you know are going to be doing bad things," said Mom. "We're not idiots, Leah. We remember. We're not the kind of parents who don't know what goes on. We just want you to be honest with us. We don't want you hiding, and sneaking, and lying. Can't we be honest? Can't we be friends?" Then she paused, as if she expected me to actually reply to that.

"Umm, okay?" I tried. Even though the moment didn't feel especially friendly.

I was trying to think of what else I could possibly say when suddenly Dad stood, picked up his travel mug and phone from the coffee table, and said coldly, "This is far from finished, young lady. But I need to leave."

Mom looked up quickly. "Paul?"

"I'm sorry, Rach. I have a meeting I can't miss. We'll have to finish this later. If you want to stay home, you should. But I . . . can't."

"But . . . ," said Mom.

"I'm sorry," said Dad, not sounding very sorry. "Life doesn't stop because Leah decides to suddenly become a juvenile delinquent. People are counting on me. I have a job to do."

"Yeah," said Mom. "I know that." Then she reached for her coffee mug on the table in front of her, and held it tightly in both hands, until the door shut with a click.

I looked at the mug. It read, *I'd rather be smashing the*

patriarchy. Then I glanced up at Mom. Her face was angry, but somehow I could tell that she was more pissed at Dad than she was at me. Only I wasn't sure what to do with that.

So I shrugged. "Toilet paper emergency," I said.

"Not funny, Leah," snapped Mom. Even though it kind of was.

Somewhere in my brain, beyond everything that was happening now, I wondered if she knew about the cornfield in the garage. I wondered if she knew why he was painting it. I wondered if Mom and Dad talked to each other, about real things. It was hard to know exactly who was lying, and exactly what about. Which was worse: a lie or a secret?

"Dammit," said Mom, startling me. She took a deep breath. "Dammit, dammit, dammit. Where *were* you, Leah? What on earth were you doing, running around the streets in the middle of the night?"

"I was . . . at a friend's house," I said. It was the truth.

Mom frowned. "Does your *friend* have a name?"

"Jasper," I said. "I told you about her, remember?"

"Yes," said Mom. "Jasper, the new friend. The girl we still haven't met. You went swimming. You painted her room." Then she added, "I need to ask. Are you sleeping with her? Or maybe the two of you went to hook up with some boys together?"

"What?"

"Or drinking? Or drugs? Are you doing drugs with her?"

"Mom!" I said. "I'm thirteen."

"Do you think we're stupid? We know what can happen. We know what kids do. We aren't fools. Kids younger than you are out there doing—"

"Mom." I cut her off. "We were just *talking*. I don't . . . *sleep* . . . with anyone. I've never even kissed anyone. Jeez. And I don't do drugs. I'm not an idiot."

"In the middle of the night, Leah? Why on earth would you sneak out for no reason, when you can see your friend anytime, all day long?"

"It just seemed . . . fun," I said. "To be out at night."

"Fun," Mom repeated. "And what kind of parents does this girl have? To be fine with you showing up randomly at that time of night? If some kid showed up here at midnight, you can bet your ass I'd call her mother and check in."

"It's complicated," I said, borrowing Jasper's words. "I don't know how to . . . explain."

"Try," said Mom.

"I want to, but—"

"Try!" shouted Mom suddenly, banging her cup down on the coffee table. There was a sharp crack, and the cup fell into two pieces, broken.

"Mom!" I said, jumping up.

I think she even surprised herself. Mom wasn't a yeller or

a smasher. I'm not sure I'd ever heard her shout like that in all my life. In that moment, it felt like *she'd* cracked. Broken, like the mug. We both stared at the handle in her hand and the other chunk of ceramic, now fallen off the table. There was coffee everywhere.

"I loved that mug," she said under her breath.

"I did too," I said.

Mom took a deep breath. "Okay, Leah. Let's try this again. I want you to explain."

She wasn't even trying to clean up the mess. She was still clutching the handle, but there was no mug attached. It was just something to hold on to.

I stood there, staring down at my mother. I wasn't sure what I was supposed to do. I'd sworn to Jasper I wouldn't tell anyone about her situation, but nothing was making any sense at all. I wished I could see her, right now. I wished I could tell her about this mess. Ask her what to say.

"Mom," I tried again. "I didn't do anything bad, I swear. I was just . . ."

Mom looked like she was going to cry, but she sounded angry, not sad, when she suddenly said, "Give me your phone, Leah, now. I don't want you scheming with this Jasper kid again until I've had a chance to meet her. *And* her parents."

"I don't have my phone on me. I forgot it when I went out."

"Then go get it. And bring it here. And your laptop too.

To begin with, you've lost screen privileges for the foreseeable future. I'm not sure what else."

So I ran to get the phone from where I'd left it beside my bed, and my laptop from my desk. As I walked back to the living room, I checked the phone. Seventeen missed calls. One after another. All from Mom.

"Here," I said, setting both devices down on the dry part of the table. "Mom. I'm sorry. But I swear, nothing bad happened. Nothing bad is happening."

Tiredly, she shook her head at me. Like she was saying *no* to the apology and *no* to me and *no* to the broken mug and the puddle of cold coffee and everything else in the world. "Go to your room, Leah. Just go to your room."

I nodded and turned to head off down the hall. But I only got about halfway to my room before I stopped and looked back at my mom. She was sitting with her head in her hands now. She wasn't crying. She was frozen.

And I couldn't do it, couldn't slip away and let the room go silent. Couldn't pretend things were fine when they weren't at all. "Mom," I called out. "It's not fair. It's not fair for you guys to only be my parents when you're mad at me, but be ghosts the rest of the time."

"What?" She lifted her head from her hands. There were tears in her eyes. "What did you just say to me? I want you to repeat that."

"I . . ." I couldn't stand the look on her face. It made my

stomach ache. "I forget. I mean, I don't know."

"No," she said coldly. "I don't think you *do* know. Now go straight to your room."

"Okay," I said. And this time I did. I walked straight to my room and crawled into bed, fully dressed. I closed my eyes and disappeared.

IN THE JUNK DRAWER

W hen I woke up a few hours later, I didn't quite remember everything that had happened. Maybe it was just too much for me, the crazy night with Jasper, followed by the fight with Mom and Dad. It felt like my brain had overloaded.

Then I looked down and realized I was still wearing my dirty clothes from the day before, and . . . bit by bit, memories began to wash over me. I lay still, sprawled and staring, trying to recall everything, to fit it all together. I thought about Jasper, back in the Vine Realm. Had she slept? She must have. If she was awake now, she was probably wondering what my parents had done to me. She was probably waiting for me to turn up. I wondered how long it would be before she came knocking on my bedroom window.

In the hallway beyond my door, I could hear Mom pacing in her ratty slippers. Every once in a while, she'd shuffle my way, stand outside the door to my room for a minute, as though she wanted to knock. But then she'd shuffle away again. I felt like I should call out to her, but I wasn't sure what I could say that wouldn't make things worse. I definitely didn't know how to fix us. We were broken. Our family was cracked all the way through, like Mom's dumb coffee mug.

I tried to force myself to go to sleep, but there was morning light streaming in my window, and as tired as I was, I only felt more awake, lying there. Finally, I did something I hadn't done in years. I bent my knees, pivoted my body, and planted my feet on the wall beside my bed. One foot at a time, I walked up the wall, with my arms braced under my back, until my feet were up near the ceiling and my back was arched. It felt strangely good to be upside down. It also felt like I was a little kid again. Sam and I had done this together, back when we still shared a room. It had been a contest, to see who would fall first. Almost always, Sam lost, but he was such a good sport about it. I remembered how it felt to be upside down, my face turning red. I remembered telling Sam jokes, so that he'd laugh and fall first.

I let my back go limp and flopped down hard on the bed. Thunk and rattle . . . I sat up and peered around my room. What was I going to do all day? No phone. No computer. No TV. Nobody to talk to. Until who knows when. What was I going to do all day? Lie there, going crazy?

I got out of bed and changed into a clean pair of shorts and a fresh shirt. Then I wandered around for a minute, looking out the window, staring at the furniture, trying to think of something to do. At last, I walked over to the bookshelf, to see if there was anything I wanted to reread, but nothing looked good. Half the books were super old. *Ivy & Bean*. *Toys Go Out*. Baby books. I should have gotten rid of them by now.

I sat on the floor in front of my bookshelves, and one by one, I started to pull the little-kid books down and stack them. For a while I stayed distracted like that, leafing through the books as I sorted them. When I was finished, I only had two shelves of books left that I wanted to keep. Around me, the floor was covered with old paperbacks.

Next, I turned my attention to the walls, which were covered with posters and framed prints and other stuff that had been there forever. All of which suddenly seemed absurd to me. This room would never be the Vine Realm, but the unicorn cross-stitch Mom had made me when I was in kindergarten was an embarrassment. The *Moana* poster I'd saved up for and bought myself at the school book fair seemed totally ridiculous to me now. I walked across the room, tore down Moana, and folded her up until the folds were too thick and I couldn't fold anymore. Then I shoved the poster in the trash. After that, I took down every piece of art and stacked it all on the floor, until the walls were bare and white, except for the streaks and scrapes and paint chips I had never noticed before.

I rummaged in my closet, and tossed every too-small sweater and shoe and pair of pants out onto the floor of my room. I tossed out my stupid yellow duck-suit pajamas. I tossed out the princess Halloween costume Mom had made me in second grade. Why was it still in there? When the closet was done, I moved on to my dresser. Old socks, threadbare tights, the jeans with a hole in the knee.

At some point, I noticed that while I'd been cleaning out the clutter, I'd also been making a gigantic mess. For some reason, the piles of books and clothes made me want to scream, so I stripped the top sheet off my bed, laid it on the floor, and moved everything onto the sheet, building a mountain of cast-offs in the middle. Then I rolled the sheet up, with all the stuff in it, like a big burrito of junk, and shoved it under my bed.

The only thing left to do now was my desk. So I sat in my swivel chair and gave myself a good quick spin before I reached down and opened all the drawers one at a time. Into the trash went dried-out markers and broken pencils. Half-used notepads and useless glue sticks.

Last of all, I reached to open my junk drawer. The place for everything that didn't have a place. When I pulled on the handle, the drawer was still jammed, but then I took a ruler from my desk and wedged it into the slit at the top of the drawer, started shoving and ramming at the stuff inside until I felt something give and the drawer shot open.

I peered inside warily. It was stuffed to the top, and I was a little afraid there might be sharp objects, rotting food. But after a minute, slowly, I began to pull everything out. One object at a time. I couldn't remember why I'd saved most of them in the first place. Corks and acorns and binder clips. Rocks I'd found in places I could no longer recall. Seven pairs of cheap plastic sunglasses, swag from booths at the East Atlanta Strut, and three totally deflated but still tied balloons at the ends of sad ribbons. Two strands of cheap purple beads. Wrappers from lunchbox cookie packs that I was only ever supposed to take for lunch but sometimes stole from the kitchen and snuck into my room to munch on late at night. I found a two-year-old permission slip from a field trip to the planetarium. And all of these things—every single one—went into the trash can under my desk.

Then I found it. At the bottom of the drawer, in the lower right-hand corner.

Technically, it was called Le Tooter. That was what the box it had come in said. Sam had shouted it at us enough times. "I'm a big pooter, with Le Tooter!" But Dad only ever called it *the Damn Fart Machine*. Sam had loved this awful thing. He'd gotten it for Hanukkah a year and a half ago from Grandpa Dan on a rare visit from Des Moines. Sam had taken it everywhere. The car, the park, the dinner table. He'd had it confiscated at school. But then . . . I'd stolen it.

How had I forgotten this? I'd stolen it the day before we

left for camp! I just hadn't been able to stomach the idea of that horrible thing, that dumb plastic noisemaker, farting away in the woods, at the lake, by the campfire. I knew it would embarrass me, so I'd stolen it from Sam's bedside table and hidden it away in my junk drawer.

I stared at it in my hand and remembered Sam, dashing around the house, as we loaded the car to leave for camp. "I'm not going without Le Tooter!" he'd cried.

"Like fun, you're not," Dad had said with a grin. And he'd picked Sam up and carried him, kicking, to the car. It had all been a joke. A big, silly joke. I'd followed the two of them out to the car, where Mom was waiting. I'd been laughing too. Except that now I remembered what else Dad had said. "*The Damn Fart Machine* will be waiting for you when you get back. *The Damn Fart Machine* isn't going anywhere."

Now I turned *the Damn Fart Machine* over in my hand. I stared at it. I pushed the button, and out came the stupid sound I remembered so well. *Thbbbbt!*

"Oh, God," I said. "Oh, God, Sam."

I didn't even try to stop myself from crying this time. It felt good to cry alone. There, in my empty room. Heavy sobs. Big and loose. Like running very fast down a hill, when you can't stop your feet even if you try. It was like I'd flipped a switch the night before, and now I couldn't turn myself off. I cried about Sam, and I cried about being in trouble. I cried about losing my phone, and not seeing Jasper. I cried because the

191

walls were so bare and the house felt too quiet. I cried because of everything, everything, everything. I cried myself limp.

Just as I was getting to that shuddering place, when the crying is stopping but your face is still all wet, the door opened and my mom peeked her head around the corner.

"Leah?" she said, opening the door a little wider. "Are you . . . ?"

I held the toy out to her in my hand. "I found this," I blubbered. *"The Damn Fart Machine."*

"Oh, dear," Mom said. She walked over to stand beside me and put a hand gently on my head. "Oh, honey."

I wiped my face with an arm. Mom was blurry through my tears. I took a deep breath. "I'm *not* in trouble. I swear I'm not doing anything bad."

"I want to believe that," she said. "I really do."

"Please, Mom," I said. "Please don't say I can't see Jasper. She's my best friend. And I was so . . . lonely." On that word, I shuddered. "Before I found her, I mean. I've been so lonely, ever since . . ."

Mom knelt down beside my chair, and it seemed for a minute like she might cry too. There was something careful and fragile about her too, as though she thought she might shatter if she moved too fast. But she didn't cry, only pushed a piece of hair out of my wet face, and then she sighed. "Look, Leah," she said. "Even if you're not doing anything *bad*, you could still get in a lot of trouble. Bad things happen to good kids."

"I know," I said. "But I'll be careful, and—"

"*Serious* trouble," she said. "It scares me. You sneaking out, like that. It's not safe. And it's my job to keep you . . . safe."

"But—"

"Maybe Jasper isn't a bad influence, and maybe she is. Maybe you've learned a lesson and you'll never sneak out again. Maybe she's a good kid, the best in the world. But if you want to spend time with her, I'll need to meet her. . . ."

I nodded furiously, sniffing back tears. "Okay," I said. "Okay."

"And also her mother," said Mom. "That's just a rule. This is not some weird idea I came up with, Leah. It's a standard-issue Mom rule."

"But it's . . . complicated," I said.

Mom stood. Not so soft anymore. She stepped away from me. "No, it really isn't. In fact, it's very simple. This is a normal request, and any good mom would do the same. I'm your mother, Leah. I love you best and know you best."

I couldn't figure what else to say. In one way, I knew she was right. It *was* normal for her to want to meet Jasper. To want to call Jasper's mom. Maybe even have her over for dinner. I could picture what my mom thought might happen. Two moms, laughing and gabbing and momming it up. I could imagine the conversation. *These girls, what are we going to do with them, always up to something!* But that conversation was never going to happen.

And the other thing was that Mom *didn't* know me best, not anymore. She hadn't bothered to know me since last summer. She didn't know Tess and I weren't friends anymore. She didn't know Jasper, and she didn't know the Vine Realm. She didn't know any of the things that mattered most to me. Even if the Vine Realm wasn't technically safe, nothing had ever *felt* so safe to me. I wished I were there, right now. Sitting on the steps, or on Jasper's bed. Drinking a warm root beer and laughing. But the only way that would ever happen again was if I did as Mom said.

I dried my face on my shirt and stood up, faced her. "Okay, then," I said. "I'll bring Jasper around. Tomorrow. If you'll let me go get her. She doesn't have a phone, so I can't call."

Mom nodded. "I suppose that would be fine. You do seem to be taking this seriously."

"I am," I said. "I promise."

"And then," said Mom, "once we've met, Jasper can put me in touch with her mother, and we'll get this all sorted out. Okay? Deal?"

Right away, I nodded. It was a lie, and it was easier to nod, for some reason, than say the lie out loud.

Mom pushed the same piece of my hair out of my face again and sighed. "Oh, Leah. This is all just because I love you. We both love you so much—your dad and me. You know that, right?"

"Sometimes," I said.

"What?" Mom sat up stiffly. "What do you mean? You only know it sometimes? Or you think we only love you sometimes?"

I shrugged. "Both?"

"C'mon, Leah. You know better. We *always* love you, with everything we have, all the time."

"You're saying that," I said, shaking my head, "but it doesn't feel like it. I mean, I *know* it, I guess. Because that's what parents are supposed to do. And I remember what it used to be like. But we're never . . . like we used to be. It doesn't feel like love. You're just nervous all the time. And Dad . . . he barely talks to me. He just lives in his phone all day. I'm not sure he remembers my name sometimes."

Mom stared at me dead-on, like she was trying to send me a message. "Leah, your father . . . he isn't good at saying things in words. He never has been. It's hard for him, to talk about the things that matter most. Can you understand that? He has other ways of expressing his feelings."

I didn't know what to say to that. I guessed it was probably true, but I didn't know what those ways might be. If someone is expressing feelings, but nobody can understand them, does it count? Anyway, we were both tired, and I didn't really want to talk anymore, so I just nodded again. It felt like another lie, but it was all I had in me. And it was something, that she'd let me go see Jasper. It was something, that Mom and I were talking. I looked around my bare room and felt a little less terrible.

Then Mom looked around too, glanced at the bare walls and empty bookcases, but she didn't say anything. She just nodded back at me.

THE WHOLE (OTHER) STORY

I went over early the next day, as soon as Mom and Dad had left for work. I made my way up the creek to the now-familiar hole in the overgrowth. I pushed my way through, and into the Vine Realm.

Jasper was sitting in the sun, reading. She set down her book as I walked up. Her usual grin was gone. I sat down beside her.

"What happened?" she asked. "When you didn't come back yesterday, I was worried your parents had literally killed you."

"I almost wish they had," I said with a grimace. "My dad's lecture was one for the record books. I don't think he took a breath for a full hour."

"Ouch," said Jasper. "So, what's the damage?" she asked. "Are you grounded until you're thirty?"

I shook my head. "They can't exactly ground me, because they have to go to work. So they aren't there to know what I do all day."

"Good point," said Jasper. "But then, what's the punishment?"

"They took away my phone for a while," I said. "And they gave me lots of disappointed looks. Also they want you . . . to come meet my mom."

"Oh, God." Jasper's eyes went wide. "Really?"

I nodded. "Yep. You can expect some hard questions. Consider yourself warned."

"But what did you tell her about me?" she asked.

"Nothing," I said. "I promise. Only that I was with you all night, talking. They were freaked out—they thought that I was off doing terrible things with boys and drugs, if you can believe that."

"Okay, but I mean . . . what did you tell them about *me*?" demanded Jasper. "My situation?"

"I didn't tell them anything! Just that you're my friend. They know that we painted the wall of your bedroom. They know that you live in the neighborhood. So now they want to meet you."

"I think it's better if they don't," said Jasper. "It makes me nervous that they even know my name."

"Only your first name," I said. "*I* still don't even know your last name."

"Even so. *Jasper*'s not a very common name for a girl. I stand out."

"Yeah, well, it gets worse," I added. "They also want to talk to your mom."

Jasper laughed. She was holding her knees in front of her, and she rocked back and forth now. "That would be hilarious," she said. "If they met her, I don't think it would help our case."

"So then, you *do* have a mom?"

Jasper stopped rocking. She looked at me seriously and sighed. "I was going to tell you the whole story the other night, wasn't I? Right when you had to go?"

I nodded. "Yeah," I said. "I spent half of yesterday wondering about that."

"I don't know," said Jasper. "It felt so right to tell you then. It doesn't feel the same . . . now." She squinted at me in the sunlight.

"Please?"

Jasper stood up and brushed off the seat of her shorts. "Well, okay," she said. "But let's get a snack. This might require some pickles." She reached down a hand. I clasped it, and she pulled me to standing. "And also . . ."

"Yeah?" I said.

"It's Cohen."

"Cohen?"

"My last name," said Jasper. "Jasper Jenna Cohen. At your service."

"But Cohen's a Jewish name," I said. "You never said you were—"

Jasper held up a finger. "First things first. We require pickles."

Five minutes later, we were sitting on Jasper's bed, face-to-face, crisscross applesauce, the pickle jar between us. Despite the involvement of pickles, the moment felt very serious, like we were signing a pact or something. Jasper's expression was grim.

"How bad can it be?" I asked. "Worse than mine?"

"Different," said Jasper. "Plenty bad. Even if it doesn't always look like it. For instance . . ." She took a giant bite of pickle and smacked her lips. "At this very delicious moment, do I look like a child in crisis?"

I just shrugged. I wasn't sure what the correct answer was. Laughing didn't feel right.

Jasper swallowed her bite. "Before I say anything, I need to be sure you understand that this is no joke. It's super serious, and if you were to tell anyone at all, you'd seriously ruin my life. But you might also ruin other people's lives. I know it might sound like I'm exaggerating, but I'm *not*, Leah. Not at all. You get that?"

"Yes," I said. "You can trust me. I'm a vault."

"I do," said Jasper. "Trust you. But I haven't told anyone my story before either. I've had to be careful. It feels weird to say it out loud, after working so hard to keep quiet."

"I know exactly what you mean," I said.

Jasper nodded, and took a deep breath, like she was getting ready to dive underwater. "You asked about my mom. And, yes, my mom is alive. But . . . she's not a mom like your mom. She's not okay. At all. She's a mess."

"What kind of mess?" I asked.

"Like a crazy-drunk mess," said Jasper. "And not like a having-some-beers-and-dancing-barefoot-at-a-neighbor's-house mess. Like the kind of mess you see in a sad movie. Like sometimes there's an empty vodka bottle in her car because that was where she drank it. Like they took her driver's license away."

"Oh," I said.

"Once, I came home from school and I found her asleep in the yard. Not passed out, just sleeping. Snoring and everything, like she was in bed. All the other kids from the bus stop walked away really fast when they saw her. It was terrible."

"Oh, God. I'd want to run away from home too if that was my mom."

"The thing is," said Jasper, "I didn't. I didn't run away from her. My mom is only the beginning of the story. When your mom falls asleep in the yard, people notice. And people *help*. Or that's what they call it. They call the police. And then the police come and the house is a disaster or your mom is in her nightgown or whatever. And maybe not the first time, but the second or the third or the fourth, they take you away, because they think your mom doesn't know how to take care of you. And then you have to go live with someone else."

"So you went to live with your dad?"

"No," said Jasper. "My dad hasn't ever been in the picture. I have his last name and, like, some mixtapes he made for my mom when they were dating. And some pictures. Anyway, the point is, I've never met him. He got my mom pregnant and left. I think he lives in Ohio."

"Oh, so you're not Jewish, *really*?"

Jasper shook her head. "Not at all, no. Or anyway, I haven't learned anything about being Jewish. But I've always been kind of curious. And, like, whenever there's a Jewish character in a movie or something, a little flare goes up in my head, like I'm sort of connected to it, in a way. But that's not really important. Anyway, when things got really bad with my mom last year, they sent me to live with my sister, who is fifteen years older than me, and also a mess, but in a totally different way."

"What do you mean?"

"See, *she* is married to the biggest creep in the world, and they have these two kids, and he hits her."

"Hits her?"

"He hits her," said Jasper. "Not often, but enough that I saw it. More than once. And hard."

"Like, with his hand?"

"Sure, that. But also like . . . once I saw him crack her across the arm with a dog leash. Choke chain and all."

"Oh," I said. My voice sounded weird and stiff, like my throat was dried out. "I don't—"

"Yeah," said Jasper when I didn't go on. "You *don't*. But here's the thing—if you get sent to live with your mess of a sister, after they take you away from your mess of a mom, and her creep husband hits her in front of you, what do you think you're supposed to do?"

"You tell your sister to leave him?" I guessed.

"Bingo!" said Jasper. "But if you do that, your sister tells you she *can't* leave him. She's afraid she won't get to keep the kids, because he makes all the money and will have a great lawyer. So she stays with him." Jasper paused and looked at me. "You still okay?"

I was stunned. I didn't know how to respond. This was all so far past anything I'd ever experienced. These weren't kid problems. But I managed a nod.

"So after you tell your sister she needs to leave him or you'll call the cops yourself, because you can't stand to watch her get hurt like that, she tells you that if you can't stand to watch it happen, you should just leave. And after a while, that is what you do. Your sister gives you some cash and her old phone, and warns you that if you get caught, she's not taking you back. So you'd better keep your mouth shut or you're going to a group home."

"Group home?"

She nodded. "It doesn't sound very nice, does it?"

I shook my head. "The whole thing sounds really bad."

"Yep, it's very bad," said Jasper. "No doubt about it." She reached for a pickle and took a big bite.

"So, but then how'd you end up here? How'd you find *this* place?"

"It was a total accident. My sister lives over in East Lake, and after we had our last fight, I just left the house and started walking. I walked and walked and walked, down Glenwood, over the highway, and past a bunch of houses, until I ended up in East Atlanta, at the coffee shop. Joe's. The lady there was nice. She let me sit there a long time and gave me a piece of rainbow cake. I had my suitcase with me, but I don't think she even saw it, or had any idea what was going on. I think she just could tell that I was having a bad day."

"That's Dawn," I said, nodding. "She's great. She's like . . . everyone's aunt, kind of."

"Okay, so I was sitting there, and after I finished my cake, I noticed there was an old poster on the wall, about an Easter egg hunt at this farm. So I came to poke around, just because it sounded interesting, and I didn't have anything else to do. But then I was exploring, and I found this abandoned house, and it seemed like maybe I could hang out here for a while, until I figured out what to do. Then I met you! My fairy godsister. And you fed me and fixed this place up and I'm not sure what would have happened if you hadn't stumbled along the creek that day. And that is pretty much the whole story. The End."

She sat there, staring at me.

"I . . . I can't . . . ," I began. "I don't even know what to say."

Jasper shrugged. "I'm not sure there's really anything *to* say."

"Have you talked to your sister since you left?"

"Yeah, I FaceTimed her the day after I left. The first night alone was really hard. I just wanted to talk to someone, you know?"

I nodded. "I can imagine, kind of."

"I could tell she felt bad. She said I could come by for cash, if I need it. And I guess I will. But it doesn't fix anything, not really."

"I just . . . I don't know how you ever feel better with all that hanging over you. Like, here you are eating pickles and enjoying them, even though you have this in your head, the whole time."

Jasper chewed for a moment. "I guess sometimes you just

do feel better. Like, you make a new friend or get a free piece of cake or enjoy a pickle, and that's enough to make things feel okay for a while. Just because things are hard doesn't mean life isn't still full of good things. Right? The same way your brother died, but the pickles are still good to you too."

"I guess," I said.

"Like, this *place*"—she threw her hands around her— "is still beautiful, no matter what else is going on. Mostly I remember that."

"And when you can't remember that? When it's too hard?"

"When it's too hard, well . . . you play the sad game."

"What's that?"

Jasper shifted herself, got up on her knees. "It's something my mom taught me to do. This one night at bedtime, I was sad about something, just in the normal little-kid way. Because someone wouldn't play with me at school or whatever. You know, like that?"

"Sure," I said.

"I went downstairs, and my mom was sitting there, listening to music in the living room, and I told her I was sad, and she said that, sometimes, fighting the sadness is worse than the sadness itself, because you just can't win. And at those times, you play the sad game. Which is just trying to let yourself be sad. To be okay with being sad."

"That doesn't sound like much of a game," I said.

"I know," said Jasper. "But it actually kind of works, if you do it right. Like, that night, my mom put on this super slow song by a guy named Leonard Cohen, about a dove who keeps getting caught and sold. And she turned out the lights, and we lay there in the darkness on the couch together, listening to the sad moany song, and telling each other the saddest things we could think of. I fell asleep right there. And when I woke up in the morning, my mom was still holding me, and I couldn't remember why I'd been so sad."

"Huh," I said. "That story is sweet. I'm not sure my mom would spend all night on the couch with me."

Jasper nodded. "Well, to be fair, she was probably drunk. But it's a nice memory. I think about it whenever I play the sad game alone, here at night. I go out on the porch and look at the trees blowing in the sky, or I listen to the cicadas, and I remember my mom, and just sort of sit with it all. I think it's kind of funny, that one of my favorite memories started out so sad."

"In that story, your mom doesn't sound like I imagined her, just now, when you told me about her."

"I get that," said Jasper. "But the thing is that just because someone is in bad shape doesn't mean they can't also be smart or nice, or that you can't also love them."

I thought about that for a little while.

"Well," I finally said, "I'm glad you love her, and I'm glad you have the sad game, but if you're really stuck here, and this is your best option, what will you do in September, when it's time to go back to school? Or in winter, when it gets super cold?"

Jasper shook her head. "I haven't gotten that far yet. This all happened a few days before I met you. I guess I've been trying not to think too much. It makes my head hurt."

"It makes my heart hurt," I said.

"That too," said Jasper.

"Maybe something will just happen? Maybe something will change."

"What could change?"

"I don't know, exactly. Like maybe your mom will quit drinking."

Jasper snorted. "Not likely. I spent years wishing for that, back when I was little enough to believe in wishes and magic."

"Well then, maybe your sister's terrible husband will get hit by a car or something. Maybe he'll just . . . die. That happens—"

My words caught in my throat, and Jasper winced at them. "You know, I *have* wished for that too. Of course I have. But it doesn't work. And it's like a kind of poison, to wish for something like that. It makes me feel bad, like *I'm* bad. Maybe I am, for thinking it. But even if that's not true, waiting around, hoping something will just change suddenly and fix all your problems . . . that's dumb. That's like being five years old and believing in fairies. Or miracles. It's better to be realistic. It's better to accept the facts and the rules, and just keep going. That's what grown-ups do."

"I guess so," I said. "Sometimes I wish for Sam to not be gone anymore. But I know some things just aren't possible."

"Right," said Jasper. "Exactly."

"But then, don't you think you should tell someone? A safe person, who might be able to find you somewhere better to stay? I mean . . . you could talk to my parents. Really. They're not the greatest, but my mom might—"

"No!" said Jasper. "No telling your *parents*."

"O-okay," I said, nodding. Jasper spit out that word, *parents*, like it tasted bad. But, lame as they were, my parents were still the people I'd call if I was sick or in trouble, I thought. Parents were safe.

"Then how about someone else?" I offered. "Maybe someone like Dawn, a cool nice grown-up? Maybe you could work at Joe's—"

"No!" shouted Jasper so forcefully I blinked. "You tell Dawn and Dawn tells the police, and that is how my sister and my mom both end up arrested. No parents and nobody else either. No way. You have to swear you won't say a word. I'm not kidding, Leah."

"Okay, okay!" I said. "It's just that now I'm . . . worried. You can't do this alone. Not forever."

Jasper shrugged. "I don't seem to have any options. Do I?"

I couldn't think of any, and we both sat there for a little while, silent. "Well maybe you *will* do it alone, and it will all work out. And someday, maybe this will be an amazing story to tell to your kids. Like the kind of story you read about in books or see in movies."

"Yeah, maybe," said Jasper, though she didn't sound convinced.

"And if *that's* true," I said, "maybe this is actually all a weird kind of fate. You know? You struck out on your own and began an incredible journey."

"What do you mean?" asked Jasper.

"I don't know. Like, all that stuff happened to you, and it's terrible for sure. But if it hadn't happened, and you hadn't left your sister's house, then you wouldn't have come here, and discovered the Vine Realm, and we wouldn't have met. And who knows where this will all end? So in a way . . . it's good that those things happened. You know what I mean?"

Jasper didn't answer at first. She just stared at me.

"No, Leah," Jasper finally said. "No, I *don't* know what you mean, not even a little bit." The look on her face was one I hadn't seen before, and her voice was cold. "Are you serious? You think maybe it's a *good thing* that my mom is a raging alcoholic and my sister will be smacked around for the rest of her life? Just so we can hang out in this old house and paint a wall?"

"No!" I said. "No, I just . . . I didn't mean it like that. I wasn't saying it's a good thing exactly. I meant . . ." I didn't know how to explain it. "I just meant I'm glad we're friends. That's all. I'm glad I met you."

"Well, sure!" said Jasper. "But by your logic, it's also a *good thing* that you ignored your brother when he needed you at the lake, so he could drown, and you'd be alone this summer, and we'd meet and eat pickles together. Is *that* what you meant?"

I felt myself go numb. My body shuddered. Briefly, I thought I might hit Jasper. Not on purpose. But it was as though my hands would suddenly just leap up on their own.

"I . . . I . . . I . . ." I couldn't find the words.

Jasper sat back. "I shouldn't have said that," she said in a whisper. "It was too much. I'm sorry. I lost my temper. I shouldn't have . . ."

I stood up from the mattress. "I think I need to go home now."

"Leah, don't—"

"No," I said. "I see what you mean. You're right. It's *not* a good thing. It's not a good thing at all."

I slid my shoes on.

"Leah, wait," said Jasper. "Please?"

But I didn't look back. I left the house, walked out the door, and didn't bother to close it behind me. I ran blindly, and slid down the hill, scraping my knee on a stump. Then through the creek until I hit Berne Street. After that I stumbled in the direction of home.

I wasn't sure what exactly had just happened. I only knew it hurt.

THE SAD GAME

The next morning was unbearable. I opened my eyes and immediately thought I might vomit. I stared around me at the bare walls, at the bare shelves. It felt like my life was disappearing.

As I lay there, my face in a pillow, I couldn't decide whether I felt more angry or more guilty. I waffled back and forth between those two feelings, and it didn't really seem to matter which I landed on. They both felt terrible. It didn't matter which one of us was to blame. We had broken the Vine Realm. We had broken everything, and I was back to being a lonely girl in a silent house.

The only way I could think of to escape myself was to slip into someone else's story and away from my own. To travel someplace where friends didn't hurt each other and brothers didn't drown and sisters didn't ever get hit and parents didn't leave or drink or go silent. Or where, when things like that happened, there was a way to solve them. I wanted to go to Hogwarts or Narnia, to someplace where broken things could magically be unbroken. Where there were wishes and potions and answers to all the mysteries. I wanted TV.

So at last I crawled out of bed and into the living room. Then for hours, I sprawled on the couch under the red blanket, covered in cookie crumbs and popcorn kernels. I couldn't seem to think of anything I really wanted to see, so instead I just flipped channels, mostly catching glimpses of boring house renovation shows and cartoons for babies. But after a while, I landed on a weird old movie I didn't recognize. On the screen, two guys were walking across a baseball diamond next to a cornfield. I sat up.

It wasn't the kind of thing I would ever watch on purpose, but I found myself frozen with the clicker in my hand. Staring at the cornfield, which looked so much like Dad's mural. The two men walked around for a while, talking about how beautiful it was there, almost like they were in love. Meanwhile the light was all glowy and hazy, which made me think I was probably right about them being in love.

Then they stopped walking, and one of them turned to the other and said, "Is this heaven?" in a real serious intense way. When he did, for some reason, my gut knotted. I gasped.

"It's Iowa," said the other guy. And then the music started swelling like movie music does when you know you're supposed to care a lot about what's happening, and that made me feel like crying, so I turned the TV off.

Once the room was silent, I thought about how unfair it was that I'd spent so many hours distracted. Jasper was probably wishing she could do the very same thing, fall into movies all day, only she didn't have any way to escape herself. I could hide from my memories, maybe. I could bury myself in blankets, disappear. Jasper couldn't.

Because what she had said was true—she was still in the middle of her disaster, and as far as I could tell, she was stuck. There was no end in sight for her. I couldn't—no matter how I tried—imagine a way for her story to right itself. It was more than I could handle even to think about it, and Jasper had to live it—had to wake up in it each morning and go to sleep in it each night. How did she do it, and keep smiling like she did?

So I decided I'd try to play Jasper's sad game, and turned the TV back on. I found the song she'd been talking about on YouTube, and then I turned out the lights and closed the blinds and lay on the couch, listening to it.

It was a sad song for sure, about widows and wars and stuff. But also it wasn't a sad song at all. "There is a crack," the song said, ". . . a crack in everything. That's how the light gets in." I thought about that—about the light that shines through broken things. I found myself listening to the song over and

215

over. And for some reason the thought of light getting in made me think about that Iowa movie with the two guys in love, and heaven, and cornfields. And *that* made me think about the garage, of course, and Dad. Which got me wondering what it felt like for him, to paint something like that, to look up and see his thoughts on the ceiling. I wondered if maybe that was Dad's version of the sad game. And even though my thoughts were all muddled and didn't make much sense, I found myself feeling a little better. Because at least I wasn't thinking about fighting with Jasper.

Late in the afternoon, I dragged myself off the couch and got dressed. Because eventually, my parents were going to come home, and I'd need to act like a normal person for an hour or two. But when a car pulled into the drive, it was Dad, alone, and he said that Mom had a late meeting, and we were on our own for dinner.

Then we both just sort of stood there, waiting for each other to do something. Dad and I didn't spend much time alone together, and while Mom wasn't a ton of fun to be around lately, she did manage to get dinner together most nights and force us all to sit down at the table. Left alone, Dad and I didn't really know how to handle dinner or each other.

"Well," said Dad. "How about I see if I can rustle up something from the freezer?" He turned around and opened the freezer drawer, began rooting around in it. "Want a burrito?"

Standing there, hunched over the freezer, holding up a

frozen burrito, Dad had never looked so tired to me. I wasn't sure how a back could look tired, but somehow it did. Dad's blue striped button-down looked tired. The faded impression of his wallet in his pants pocket looked tired. All of it, tired. In the glare of the bright kitchen light, I noticed that his hair was getting thin in the back. I could see his pale scalp through it.

"I'm not very hungry."

He turned around and stood up. "Oh, really?"

"No. In fact, I think I might just go to my room."

"If you want, we could get pizza or something. Or call for Indian? Does any of that sound good?"

"You can," I said, "I'm not hungry."

He was trying. I could tell he was trying. But I just didn't think I could sit at the table with him tonight, not talking, all by ourselves. I'd *not* ask him about the mural, and he'd *not* answer me. I'd *not* tell him about Jasper, and we'd *not* talk about Sam. It was really exhausting, I'd found, *not* talking.

For a minute, staring at his stubbly face, his broad square shoulders, I remembered how big he used to seem to me. Like the strongest man in the world. He used to let me climb him—he'd grab my hands and I'd plant my little feet on his shinbones and walk straight up his body, all the way into his arms. That seemed like an impossible memory now, something I'd dreamed up.

"Well," he said suddenly, "if you don't want anything special, I guess I'll just have myself a sandwich."

I nodded and waved and left the room, feeling a mixture of relief and guilt. I put my pajamas back on, climbed into bed, and turned the lights out, wishing I could fall right to sleep, escape this horrible day. Maybe, somehow, I'd feel better tomorrow. Maybe things would magically change.

But a little while later, still awake, I was thirsty, and so I padded down the hall, back to the kitchen. When I did, I found my father sitting alone at the table. Most of the lights in the room were off. Just the lamp above the stove was burning, a yellow glow, casting shadows. He looked up when I stepped into the room. "Oh, hello again," he said. "Fancy seeing you here."

"Ha," I said. It was a pretty sorry excuse for a joke.

In front of my dad sat a glass of water and a small plate, holding a mostly eaten sandwich. I thought it was probably the saddest dinner of all sad dinners.

"What kind of sandwich?" I asked.

"Peanut butter on wheat," he said with a sigh.

"No jelly?"

"No jelly. We were out."

I took a glass from the cabinet and filled it at the tap. It felt like I was moving in slow motion. It felt like my brain was empty. There was nothing to say.

But then I turned. "Dad?" My voice came out shaky. I didn't have any words for what I wanted to say to him. What I really needed was help. What I really needed was for someone to tell me what to do. What I really needed was for him to drive me over to the farm. And then to solve everything, the way parents are supposed to solve everything.

I needed for him to be my dad. Right now. This minute! But when he looked up, his eyes were lost. Everything in the world was lost.

"Yes, Leah?" he said quietly.

I opened my mouth to speak, but then I shut it, and we both stared at each other, as if there was a conversation waiting for us, floating in the air around us, and one of us only needed to reach up and catch it.

At last I said, "Never mind."

He reached for his phone. "Okay."

About an hour later, Mom still wasn't home, and I was still wide-awake. That's when, in the dark stillness of the house, I heard the back door open. Carefully, I slipped out of bed and down the hall. From where I stood, I could see that the kitchen light was still on. Then I heard the screen door settle quietly, as if someone had gently closed it, not just let it bang shut like usual. I sneaked forward into the kitchen, drew aside the curtain at the back window, and watched as the garage door opened and a rectangle of dingy yellow light beamed out into the night. The door closed. The light disappeared. And swallowed up my dad.

My dad. Silent. Always disappearing.

In a heartbeat, everything inside me was different. As though someone had thrown a switch. Suddenly, all the guilt I'd been carrying was gone. All the glassy fear, the held breath, gone. In its place was thunder building. A rumble of anger. A match striking. It felt like all I needed to do was open my mouth, and flames would burst out. I looked over and found I was pulling on the curtain beside me. Tugging at it, hard. In fact, it was ripping at the seam.

I let go and let the curtain fall. Then I opened the back door. In bare feet and pajamas, I padded out after him, on cracked concrete and dead leaves. I nearly cried out when I stepped on an acorn cap. I stumbled to the door, and before I could lose my nerve, I flung it open.

But when I looked inside, Dad wasn't painting. He was just sitting there, on the blue tarp, crisscross applesauce, like a kid. He was slumped forward. His head was in his hands. And he was crying. Silently, but shaking, with big heaving sobs.

He had to know I was there. The door had made a big bang when I opened it, but he didn't look up. He just sat there, crying, alone. Stoop shouldered. Broken. And just like that, my thunder was gone. My flames fizzled.

Dad.

There was a part of me that wanted to go and sit with him, wanted to pat his back, or give him a hug. There was a part of me that wanted to cry too, wanted to ask him the questions I'd been thinking about all day, all year. A part of me that could remember how he used to be, and hoped that if I said the right words, maybe he could be that dad again.

But I don't know what might have happened if I'd stepped forward. I'll never know. Because there he was, ignoring me completely, pretending I hadn't opened the door. So I decided to pretend too. I turned and left, walked back out into the driveway. Where I stepped on the same dumb acorn cap, all over again.

Or maybe it was a different acorn cap. It didn't really matter.

LIKE ANY DAY

The next morning, I woke up hollow. Hungry feeling. Inside myself, I couldn't find the storm anymore, the thunder. But the tight cold feeling was gone too, the guilt. I felt strangely loose. Ready. And I knew exactly what needed to happen next. Sleep had cleared my head, so I grabbed a granola bar and headed to the farm. To Jasper.

My father might never be ready to turn around, face me. But that didn't mean I wasn't right to open the door. And Jasper deserved that chance too. It wasn't fair to leave her in that hot room alone, feeling guilty or hurt or abandoned. No matter what she'd said. I had her and she had me, and I wasn't going to walk away.

But as I came along the creek bed, and neared the Vine

Realm, I stumbled on a stranger, a man sitting on Sam's rock, only about twenty feet away from the gap in the kudzu that led to Jasper's house. He was homeless looking, but not in the old, sad way. He wasn't mumbling to himself or sleeping with his shirt over his head. In fact, he was young, maybe handsome. He had a guitar and an army pack on the rock with him. He had long blond hair and a deep tan. But as I neared his rock, something about the way he looked at me made me nervous. He turned to me, waved, and said, "What's up, little lady?" He winked, and I noticed his neck tattoos, all black and swirling lines.

I stopped and waved back. A careful wave—friendly, but not too friendly, I hoped. "Hi."

He grinned and took a sip from a bottle he had hidden down by his side, where I hadn't noticed it. One of his teeth was silver. It blinked in the sun.

I didn't know what to do now. I wanted the man gone. I wanted him to leave the farm and the creek, go away. But I couldn't think of anything I could possibly do to make that happen. He looked comfortable there in sun, like he had no intention of moving anytime soon. But I couldn't go to Jasper's until he left, couldn't risk showing him the path through the kudzu that led to the house.

Then, from somewhere inside me that didn't feel like my own brain, ideas formed. Words shot out of my mouth before I even knew what I was saying. The words came out loud.

"That's not your rock!" I said.

"Hey, now, mama," said the man, laughing easily. "No need to be harsh. I'm just sitting a bit."

I shook my head. "No. You can't sit there. That's my brother's rock." My voice was almost a shout. It felt big, like it was rushing out of me from somewhere deep down. "Nobody else should sit there."

"Aww, I bet your brother don't mind," said the man. "I bet he'd say it's fine."

"Well, you can't ask him," I said. "Because he's dead."

The man's eyes opened wider. He looked surprised. "Oh, sorry," he said. "That's heavy." At the same time, he was annoyed at me. I could tell. He wanted me to leave and let him drink whatever was in his bottle.

I stood my ground. "My brother died *here*," I lied, and found that the lie felt good, and strong, almost true. "On *that* rock. Right there where you're sitting. Nobody ever sits on it. If you were from here, you'd know that. Sam's ghost lives there. You should go away. Right now. It's a . . ." I searched for the words I wanted. "It's a desecration of his memory."

Now the man looked genuinely freaked out. Maybe he even thought I was a little crazy or something. He grabbed his pack and guitar with one arm and slid down the rock, bottle in hand. He splashed into the creek in his hiking boots and, in one big stride, stepped out on the other side of the creek.

"Hey, I didn't mean any harm, really," he said. And he

sounded sorry enough, maybe even kind, but now I could see that there was a gun in a holster by his side. That scared me. I'd never seen a gun up close before. My parents hated them, and I wasn't allowed to go to houses where parents even owned them.

I pretended not to see the gun, or I tried not to see it. I tried not to stare at it. "Go away," I said, my eyes focused on his. "Go away and never come back here."

The man put up his hands in a funny gesture, almost like he was doing some sort of apology dance. "Hey, it's cool, it's cool." He turned to walk away along the creek bed before he added, "Want some friendly advice, little lady? You might try being a little kinder to strangers. Karma, you know?" Then he winked, and I wasn't sure what I was supposed to think of that.

I stood, my heart pounding up into my throat, and stared at the back of his black T-shirt and his tangled blond hair as he walked away. My legs trembled and my blood thrummed. I was bursting with what I'd done. What my anger had done, and my lie. Maybe a thing didn't need to be true to be powerful.

But just where the creek bent, where it opened out in the direction of the road, the man paused and looked back at me again. He gave one last wave and then pivoted, to peer up the embankment at the place where Jasper and I had been trampling down the kudzu for weeks, where the gap in the brush was more visible than I'd realized. He squinted at it, glanced back at me again, and then turned, walked quickly away.

I watched him go, waited until he was completely out of sight. Then I waited another minute or two to make sure he didn't double back before I scrambled up the hill and through the vines. I dashed up to the porch, and around the house to the back door, to Jasper.

But when I pushed it open, I found the house still and empty. "Hello?" I called faintly, and then louder. "Hello?" I poked my head into the bathroom, just in case, but it was empty too.

Without Jasper, it didn't feel the same. It wasn't the Vine Realm. It was only a hot shabby kitchen in a falling-down house. I didn't want to spend another minute there.

Walking home, I felt tangled, anxious, but I couldn't sort out exactly why. For a year, it had been like my head was full of static, like the sound of cars rushing by on the highway. That had been awful, but in a way it had been simple. The same numb ache each day. Now the static was gone, and I could hear voices again, but it was like there were three blaring televisions on at the same time, all full of shouting. I couldn't decide which of them to worry about. That's what I was trying to figure out as I neared home and turned up the walk, to a sound I hadn't heard in over a year.

Laughter. Familiar laughter. Mom's laughter. Bright bursts of it. "Hee-hee!" Even before I stepped inside, through the panes of glass in the kitchen door, I could see where it was coming from. Mom was in my usual spot. And across from her sat Jasper. They were drinking coffee, deep in conversation.

It was unbelievably strange, seeing Jasper there with my mom. Jasper always seemed larger than life to me, with her big smile and that head of curls. She was brighter than anyone else I knew. She had a shine to her. But sitting there with Mom, she looked smaller than usual, and sort of . . . normal. Like any other girl might look, with a tangle of red hair, a black T-shirt, and flip-flops. Laughing and talking with my mom. I liked it, and at the same time, it didn't feel right.

At last I stepped up to the door and reached for the knob.

They both turned at the sound of the door opening. And when she saw it was me, Mom flashed me a smile. A real smile. Easy. I hadn't seen that smile in months and months.

"Mom!" I said. "You're home early from work."

"Oh, hey, honey!" she called out. "We wondered where you'd gotten off to."

I stood in the doorway. I had no idea what Jasper had told Mom. I couldn't figure out what was happening. I didn't want to say the wrong thing and jinx us.

"Hi?" I said cautiously.

"I was just getting to know Jasper, and we're having such a nice time. I only wish you'd brought her over sooner."

"Oh . . . ," I said. "That's great."

Behind my mom's back, Jasper smiled at me, gave a slight nod. As if to say "It's okay" and also "I'm sorry" and maybe

"I forgive you" too. Most of all, the nod said, "Relax, Leah."

I tried to.

"Sit down!" Mom said. "Jasper was just asking me about work today, and I was telling her about this interview I did, with a crazy man in Newnan who rescues pythons and keeps them in his house. Hundreds of them. Can you imagine? All those snakes, walls lined with cages. Imagine the poor mice!"

"I think it's so cool that your mom is a writer," said Jasper. "She gets to go to all kinds of interesting places, huh?"

"Well, Newnan's not *that* interesting," I said. But I sat down with them and listened as Mom finished her story. I hadn't heard her talk about work in a long time. But then, I also hadn't asked her about it in a long time.

Mom kept talking about the snakes for a few minutes longer, but at last she stood up. "You girls probably have other things to do today, and anyway, I need to go to the grocery store. But, hey, can you just rinse out those coffee cups for me, Leah? Before you run along?"

She turned to the fridge and started rooting around in it, tossing out moldy produce, as I grabbed the mugs from the table. A familiar inscription caught my eye. *I'd Rather Be Smashing the Patriarchy*. When I held it up close, I could see a faint seam running down the handle, like someone had drawn a pencil line along the white mug.

"Hey, you fixed it!" I said.

Mom glanced back at me. "Of course. I've had that thing

for decades. It's hardly the first time I've cracked it. Won't likely be the last."

I ran my finger along the crack. "But you can hardly even tell it was broken."

"Well, yeah, that's why God invented Krazy Glue," said my mom with a little laugh.

As Jasper and I were leaving the kitchen, Mom turned back to us once more, a stalk of broccoli in her hand. "Hey, Jasper."

"Yeah?" Jasper said.

"Would you like to have dinner with us tonight? I'm planning on cooking a real meal for a change."

"Oh!" said Jasper. "I . . . don't want to put you out."

"It's no trouble," said Mom. "Really. And I'm sure Paul—Leah's dad—would love to meet you too."

"I'd like that," said Jasper, nodding. "But some other time? My mom told me we had plans tonight. Can I come tomorrow instead, maybe?"

"Sure," said Mom, smiling again, easy. "Or another night. Anytime."

As we settled down on my bed, I found I had no idea what to say to Jasper. I was so glad to see her, but I wasn't sure where we stood exactly. Who was apologizing to who? I didn't really care very much, but I didn't want to screw this up.

"I played the sad game," I said, after a moment. "And it worked, some."

"I did too," said Jasper.

"And I'm sorry. For what I said, about fate. But also I'm sorry if there's anything else I said that wasn't right. Maybe I wasn't totally ready for everything you told me. I didn't realize how serious it would be."

Jasper nodded. "I get it. And I'm sorry too, for what I said, about Sam."

"It's okay," I said, and it was, now. "You know what else?"

"What?"

"I'm glad we fought. I thought about it a lot last night, and I really am."

"Really?"

I nodded. "I've spent the last year not fighting or crying with anyone. I think maybe it's good to be sad, and angry. It's not fun. But it's better than *not* being sad and angry. It's better than being nothing. Does that sound crazy?"

Jasper shook her head. "Not even a little bit. Let's make a deal. Let's promise to get angry and sad when we need to, but always apologize and make up after. How's that?"

"As long as we apologize quickly," I added. "Yesterday was no fun."

"Agreed!" said Jasper. "I felt terrible all yesterday. I waited for you, and I wanted to come here, but I didn't want to get you in trouble. Then, today, I couldn't stand it any longer, and I came over. I'm glad I did too—your mom is the best. You didn't ever mention that she used to live in New York City, or that she has her nose pierced. You made her sound . . ."

"What?"

"Boring," said Jasper. "You said she was a ghost."

"Well, yeah, I guess," I said. "I mean, a boring person can have a nose ring. And New York is probably full of ghosts. But I don't know. She's just been . . . floating this year." I thought of all the pillow forts Mom had helped Sam build over the years, and all the times she'd let us eat dinner in those forts. Then there was the time she took me for a pedicure where tiny fish nibbled at my toes. Most moms didn't do those things.

"I don't know," I said, hugging my pillow as I tried to sort out what to say. "I . . . I . . . don't know how to explain."

"Explain what?"

"It's just that . . . *that* woman, the person you just talked to, that snappy excited lady . . . who told you a bunch of stories and laughed a lot? I haven't seen her in a long time. She's not like that anymore, fun and awake."

"It sure looked like she was today," said Jasper.

"Yeah, I know," I said. "Watching her today, it was almost like the end of a fairy tale. Like there was a curse and you somehow broke it. Like the prince kissing Sleeping Beauty. You woke her up."

Jasper laughed. "I promise I didn't kiss your mom."

"No, seriously," I said. "I think it's *you*. It's like she met you, and now she doesn't seem to care about meeting your mom, and you're invited for dinner, and she's all cheerful and normal. What's that all about? How'd you do that? And can you fix my dad too?"

Jasper shrugged. "If your ghost dad is anything like your ghost mom, he'll turn out to be some fascinating and hilarious rock star."

I thought about Dad, crying in the garage. His sad back. His peanut butter sandwich. "Not likely."

"Anyway," said Jasper, "what do you think she's making for dinner?"

I laughed and tossed the pillow in my hands at Jasper. "If I had to guess, I'd say something with garlic. One thing to know about my mom is that when she actually does cook, the house smells like garlic. That's one thing that *hasn't* changed since Sam died."

"Hey, better than stale peanut butter crackers," said Jasper wistfully. "I really do wish I could stay for dinner tonight, but it seemed smarter to go home. Things were going so well. I didn't want to mess it all up."

"How about this? Whatever dinner turns out to be, I'll bring you some tomorrow," I said. "Or you can come back over and have leftovers for lunch."

"Sure!" She tossed the pillow back, right at my head, got up, and headed in the direction of the bathroom.

Watching her, I felt grateful that it was so easy to be okay. That we'd been able to tell each other these terrible stories, and fight, and make up, just like that. It was like Jasper was more like family than a friend. Or, more like family than family. It was like I'd known her my entire life. Like we belonged together.

Except that deep inside me, somewhere underneath the relief, I couldn't stop thinking about Jasper's sister, about Jasper's mom, about Jasper having no home. How did she do it? How did she walk around all day, laughing and being normal, tossing pillows and drinking coffee like a regular person, when such a terrible and heavy thing was looming over her, always? I wished I could fix it for her. I wanted to take that worry away.

I thought about how Jasper had laughed with Mom at the kitchen table, how Mom had taken to her. *Maybe*, I thought, *maybe Mom could help. Maybe Jasper just doesn't know how to tell her story to a grown-up, or she hasn't met the right grown-up. Jasper doesn't know what safe feels like.* But then I remembered how she had reacted to the idea of telling anyone, how scared she was, how she was right, that there was probably no way to tell anyone what was going on without everything else tumbling down. Also, I had made a promise. Now that Jasper and I were okay again, the last thing I wanted to do was shatter everything. So I pushed away those thoughts.

"So," I asked when Jasper got back. "I have an idea for something we can do, but it's probably dumb."

"Eh, I'm okay with dumb," said Jasper. "What is it?"

"Just that the Vine Realm is so cool, and *my* walls are so

bare . . . I thought it might be neat to paint a mural on my wall too."

"Oh, that's not dumb!" said Jasper. "That's fun. Any idea what you want to paint?"

"Actually, that's the part I thought might be cheesy."

"Bring on the cheese," said Jasper.

"I thought it would be cool if, since we painted that door on your wall, maybe *I* could have a door too. Almost like . . ."

"Like the doors connect!" said Jasper right away. "Like a Portkey?"

"Yes!" I said. "Exactly. Because wouldn't it be amazing if that was true, if we could actually walk back and forth from the Vine Realm to here? To grab a sandwich or a Popsicle."

"Or a shower?" Jasper laughed.

"Yes! Like you sort of lived here, and the Vine Realm was just another bedroom, with a very long hallway leading to it. Wouldn't that be amazing?"

"So let's do it!" said Jasper.

I ran to get the paint, and for the next hour or two, we worked. Just as she had at her place, Jasper sketched the door and added the knob. Then we painted in silence, happily, until Mom knocked on the door.

"Oh! Girls," she said, looking startled. "I didn't know you'd decided to paint in here."

"It's my room!" I started to argue.

But I didn't need to—Mom was smiling. "Hey, hey, no worries, it's pretty and so creative. You know what? I bet your dad will love it. He used to do murals once upon a time. He might even want to help!"

I looked back at the mostly finished wall. "Oh, you think?" I said.

"I'd only suggest that you open a window in here, because of the fumes," Mom continued. She crossed the room and lifted the window for us.

After she'd left, Jasper stood for a minute, staring after her. "She's, like, the kind of mom I dream about, Leah. No lie." Her voice was a little rough, stuck in her throat.

"She's really not so perfect," I said. "She's mostly performing for you. I swear."

Jasper shook her head. "But even if that's true, it's *nice* that she's performing. Isn't it? She's performing to make you happy. She's performing *love*."

"I guess. . . ."

"Anyway," said Jasper, "she doesn't have to be perfect to be a good mom. She just has to be *here*."

"But that's the thing! So often she *isn't* here," I said. "She wanders around not saying *anything*, except to occasionally nag me. I swear, she's mostly a ghost mom."

Jasper stopped painting and shook her head. "No, Leah. You keep saying that, but it's just not true. Maybe she's sad.

But she's not a ghost mom. *I* have a ghost mom. You can't hug a ghost. Ghosts don't make dinner or open the window because of paint fumes. For real."

"Maybe there are different kinds of ghost moms," I said.

"Stop it!" said Jasper, throwing her paintbrush down. "Stop making your life worse than it is. I'm glad for you that you have a nice mom. *You* should be glad for you too. You don't have to relate to everything about me. You really don't."

When she said that, I suddenly knew exactly what she meant. "Oh!" I said. "Oh, wow, you're right. . . . I'm sorry."

"Nothing to apologize for," said Jasper, reaching down to pick her brush back up. "Not a big deal. Just be grateful."

"No, I mean, what you just said, about relating. It's so true. I remember how right after Sam died, people always wanted to tell me about the sad-death-thing that happened to them. But it was usually some dog dying, or a really old grandma. It made me crazy. Because that's not the same."

"Yeah, no, it isn't," said Jasper. "Not at all. But it doesn't have to be. It isn't a contest, pain. And sometimes, you can't make it go away no matter what you do. You just have to carry it around, you know?"

I nodded. "I *do* know.

"I *know* you know," said Jasper.

I laughed. "You know something else?" I said.

"What?"

"You're my best friend. Ever."

She smiled. "I know that, silly, and you're mine. But how will that go down when Tess gets back?"

"Oh," I said, realizing how long it had been since I'd really thought about Tess. "Tess."

"You never talk about her, but I swear you told me she was your best friend, didn't you?"

"She *was*," I said. "For a long time. But she just isn't anymore."

"You don't miss her?"

I shook my head. "Not really. Tess is like family. We'll still see each other. That's how Ormewood is. But when Sam died, things changed between us. I was thinking, all year, that everyone *else* had changed, and that was hard for me. But now I'm thinking maybe it's me. Maybe I've changed. And maybe that's okay."

"Really okay?"

I nodded. "Really okay."

And it was, so we went back to painting the leaves on the wall in comfortable silence.

At last, the mural was finished, and we stood back to look at it. It was even nicer than the door in the real Vine Realm. I guessed we'd learned something from our many hours of painting, gotten better as we went along. There were purple morning glories entwined with the leaves, and Jasper had painted amazing butterflies and ladybugs all over the kudzu leaves. The late-afternoon light that shone in through the open window made the whole thing come alive.

"Wow," I said. "It's really great!"

Jasper nodded. "It really is!" she said. "Maybe I want to be an artist."

"Maybe you do."

Jasper sniffed the air, which was now perfumed with the smell of something rich and meaty, but as full of garlic as promised. "God, whatever your mom is making sure smells good. Now I'm wishing I hadn't said no to dinner."

"Yeah," I said. "But I'll bring you some, I promise. Whatever it is."

She sighed. "Thanks. But I guess I should head out. You know, since my *mom* is expecting me for family dinner?"

I laughed. "Okay," I said. "But before you go, there was one more thing I wanted to tell you."

Jasper raised her eyebrows.

"It's probably no big deal, but I saw a guy hanging around the entrance to the Vine Realm earlier, when I stopped by to look for you. And he kind of . . . spooked me."

"Spooked you how?"

"I don't know. He just gave me a bad feeling. He had tattoos, and a funny tooth. I waited for him to leave before I headed up to your house, and he did leave after a while. But I still thought you should know. And be careful. He might come back."

Jasper didn't move for a moment, but then she shrugged.

"Eh. There have to be other people who know about the place. When I first moved in, I cleared out a bunch of cigarette butts and a pair of gross pants. Like, *gross* gross. But nobody's come in since I've been there. I'm not worried."

"Okay," I said.

It didn't feel totally okay, but I guessed there wasn't much to be done. And like Jasper had said, sometimes you couldn't make the bad feeling go away. Sometimes you just had to carry it. If Jasper could carry it, I could carry it too.

A CHANGE IN THE WEATHER

That night I lay in bed and stared at the new door on my wall. My portal to the Vine Realm. The room smelled faintly of paint, and there were still streaks in the winding lines of green we'd painted that glistened, as though wet, in the yellow light from the front porch on the other side of my window. I stared at the vines and wondered whether Jasper was staring at the vines on her wall too. I liked the idea that we were staring at the same thing.

Outside, it was raining again, and the sound of the rain was soft and even, whispering against the trees and drumming on the roof. Just the right kind of rain. Only I couldn't help thinking about Jasper's leaky roof and the buckets on the floor of her kitchen. I hoped she was safe and dry. I tried hard

240

not to think about the man on Sam's rock. I tried hard not to think about the door that didn't lock. I tried hard not to imagine a face at Jasper's window, peering down at her. A tooth, blinking in the moonlight. I couldn't seem to stop imagining bad things. I turned over and buried my head in the pillow, but that didn't help. I flipped back over again and stared at the portal.

Suddenly, I sat up. It was too hard not to see the pictures I didn't want to see. I shook my head, but the pictures were still there. I checked my phone. It wasn't really that late. Only about ten. But it felt later. I climbed down out of bed and walked to the door of my room, peered out. I heard voices, faint voices.

Down the hall I padded in bare feet, past the bathroom. At the end of the hallway, I stood at the kitchen door. There was light coming from the crack underneath it. I listened, waiting. Hoping to eavesdrop on something serious. Something about me. I always sort of assumed that when my parents were talking in hushed voices, it was about me.

But it wasn't, not this time.

They were just talking to each other. About their boring days. Like regular married people.

"So *then*," Mom was saying, "the guy who is *supposed* to be bagging the groceries turns to me and says, 'Hey, does this look funny to you?' And he shows me a picture on his phone of his dog. But the dog—get this—has two tails."

"That had to be some kind of joke," said Dad. "Right? Some trick? He's just trying to get a reaction. Has to be . . ."

Mom laughed. "Who knows . . . the world is so strange!"

Then Dad took a sniff, and I knew exactly what it was. Wine. He'd always done that, stuck his nose in his wineglass and inhaled before taking a sip. Mom teased him about it. She thought it was pretentious. But I hadn't heard the sound in a long time. I couldn't remember the last time my parents had just sat with a bottle of wine, together, and no TV.

"I don't know, Paul," said Mom. "He looked utterly convinced. I told him to see a vet. And then stop bagging groceries and start his own web channel, for bizarre animal deformities."

Dad laughed. "You're so gullible, Rach."

"Yeah, well, life's more fun that way."

Then there was a long pause in the conversation. So I knocked lightly on the door. One, two, three knocks, before I stepped into the room, and did that thing where I rubbed my eyes, so it looked like I was just waking up from having fallen asleep. I didn't want them to know I'd been listening. They were sitting together at the kitchen table, but not across from each other. Beside each other. Close. Her head was on his shoulder.

"Hey," I said. "You're up . . ."

"Hey!" they called out in unison, smiling. It didn't feel totally natural, the moment. It didn't feel totally right. But they both looked glad to see me.

So I smiled too. And when I opened my mouth, what came out was "Mom, I just wanted to . . . thank you."

Mom put her glass down. "For what?"

"For being so nice to Jasper today," I said.

"Oh, honey, of course!"

"I haven't had a new friend in a long time. I don't know if you know this, but Tess and I aren't . . . the same. As before. Did you know she went to camp, *my* camp?"

My mom's eyes looked tender as she nodded. "I did know, honey. I probably should have talked to you about it. It was a strange decision, I thought. I told Bev so. We spoke about it after you ran into her a few weeks ago. She was concerned for you. But I wasn't sure what to say to you, so I didn't say anything."

"It's okay," I said. "I'm okay. But mostly I'm okay because of Jasper. And I guess I was nervous about her meeting you, but she had a lot of fun with you today. It made me feel really . . ."

Mom nodded.

Dad didn't move.

For some reason, it took me a moment to finish the sentence. "Happy."

Mom blinked a bunch of times, like she had something in her eye. "Well, it made me happy too, Leah. I really liked Jasper. She seems genuinely lovely."

"She is!" I said. "I've never had a friend like her. She's special."

"I could tell," said Mom. "She seems mature for her age, and she seems to love you."

That word should have made me squirm, but it didn't. I loved Jasper too. I nodded. "Well, anyway, thank you."

"Next time she comes over, she should stay for dinner. So Dad can meet her too."

"Okay," I said, nodding. "Well, I guess that was all I wanted to say." It wasn't, of course. Things felt so soft and safe in the kitchen, better than they had in a long time, and I wanted to spill everything that was inside me. I wanted to tell them about Jasper, and her mother, and her sister. I wanted help for her, and also, I think, I just didn't want to carry the secret alone. But I didn't say any of that. I couldn't. I'd made a promise, and so I only said, "Good night."

"Good night, Leah," said Mom, as Dad took the last sip of his wine and rose to set the glass on the counter.

In that moment, the air felt electric. The kitchen windows filled with blinding light. The hairs on my arms buzzed, and a split second later, the house shuddered with a massive crash of thunder. I gasped and looked around at Mom and Dad, who both looked alarmed too. Somewhere nearby, I heard branches breaking.

And then the lights blinked off and the room was totally, totally dark.

"Oh God," I said.

"It's okay, Leah." Dad's voice was certain, soothing.

"Probably just a limb hit a power line. But it feels like that was right over the house. Let's wait a sec and see if the lights come back on."

We all stood still, in the absolute darkness, waiting. Outside, the storm sounded much louder now. Rain pummeled the window, and the panes shook from giant gusts of wind that seemed to have come out of nowhere—blowing hard, then softer, then harder again. After a minute, I heard a chair scrape against the tile.

"Mom?" I said. "Dad?"

"Right here, kiddo." A hand fell on my shoulder.

Then I heard the gas jets on the stove flare on, and Mom was lighting a candle that she'd found somewhere and walking it over to me, putting her arm on my shoulder too.

"Why don't we all just go to bed now?" said Mom in a soft voice. "It's late, and Dad and I have work in the morning. The lights are sure to come back sooner or later."

"Okay," I said.

"Sure," said Dad. "Just let me check and make sure there isn't a tornado watch first." He pulled out his phone and scrolled around in it, and for once it made me feel better to see that. "Nope," he said after a minute. "It just looks like a really bad storm. Maybe it'll pass quickly."

"Let's hope," said Mom. "Now bedtime."

So that was how all three of us walked down the hall together. Mom was on my right and Dad was on my left, and they both kept their hands on my shoulders. Connected that way, the three of us stumbled in the darkness, with our candle, until we reached my room.

Then they were tucking me into bed, both of them. Patting my head, like I was little again, but I didn't complain. I only said, "Good night."

"Sweet dreams," said Mom.

"The sweetest," said Dad.

Then they shuffled out with the candle, back to the hallway, and off to bed. Together. Arm in arm. I lay there under my covers and watched them go as the room turned to pitch. I snuggled down under the blanket and closed my eyes. I tried to sleep.

But with the power off, there was no air-conditioning, and the room quickly got hot and stuffy. Outside, the storm didn't let up. It got worse and worse as I tossed and turned, kicked off my covers. Thunder growled overhead, and wind whipped the house, spattering the window beside my bed with bullets of rain. Now and then, I heard the cracking sound of branches breaking above the house, followed by the thunk of wood hitting the roof; and each time lightning split the sky, it was so bright I could see it through my eyelids, no matter how tightly I squeezed them shut. Then, somewhere close by, a cat started yowling, and I realized I hadn't seen Mr. Face all day.

I sat up and stared through the window, searching. It was hard to make out anything at all. The clouds blocked the stars and moon, and even the streetlights were dead. But things were definitely happening out there. I could feel them. There was so much going on in the sky and the air and the trees. I heard the cat again, screaming.

So I climbed out of bed. I raised the window, and the screen too. I stuck my head out. "Mr. Face?" I shouted into the blowing wind, as rain needled my tired eyes. Even here, under the overhang of the porch, the rain was falling sharp and quick, nearly sideways.

"Mr. Face!" I didn't want to wake my parents, but I doubted anyone, including the stupid cat, could hear my call over the wild thunder and the windy night. "Here, kitty, kitty, kitty!"

No luck.

I thought again about Jasper, alone in her house. I hoped her solar battery had lasted this long. Maybe for once she had light, while I was in darkness. I tried to imagine her cozy, under the blue blanket, with lights twinkling around her. Maybe she had fallen asleep before the storm got so bad. Maybe she could sleep through it.

But no matter how I tried, I couldn't *not* think of the man. With his bottle and his gun. I couldn't *not* picture his tooth. I couldn't *not* see him in my mind, standing in the creek, peering curiously up into the Vine Realm.

I stood at the window, thinking. If I were a homeless man who'd discovered a nice little overhang, a safe embankment, and a well-trodden path into a hidden place. If I were sleeping outside, and it began to crash and rain terribly hard on a dark night, where would I go?

I looked at the sky beyond the porch, into the empty blank space above. I listened to all the sounds of the storm—the cracking and thunder and the wind, and the rain itself, beating against the tin roof of the carport like a shower of coins. The streets would be flooding. Which meant the creek would be high.

I stood up, walked to the center of the room. Probably she was fine. Probably I was imagining things. Even if the man did find the house, maybe he was nice, just a guy looking for a dry place to hole up. Maybe Jasper was sharing her pickles with him.

I shook my head. No matter how I tried, I couldn't push the pictures out. The crashing storm, tearing away pieces of Jasper's house, tossing branches onto her roof. The man, with his tooth. His gun. His glance up into the kudzu.

Deep inside myself, I felt that something was wrong.

I couldn't explain it. It didn't make any logical sense. I just *felt* it, like someone was crying so far away I couldn't really hear it, but I knew it was still happening.

How could I ignore the voice that wasn't there?

How could I do that . . . again?

How could I ignore this feeling? How could I look away? Here I was, in my safe dry room. Back on the raft. Meanwhile,

Jasper was out there, floating, alone . . .

I jumped as the lightning flashed again, and it lit up my room, illuminating the painting on the wall. My portal. The door that wasn't a real door. Couldn't be . . .

Only somehow, in the gleaming flash of the moment, the door looked different. Now the vines looked greener, brighter, more entwined. The brown door looked different too—rougher, as though made from old splintered wood. And the knob. The knob shone, glossy and polished. As though made of actual brass, as though I might actually be able to . . .

It wasn't possible.

I couldn't be possible.

And yet . . .

So I ran. I ran at the door. I bounded, crossed the room in three steps. Breathless, I reached out an open hand, stretched my fingers, wishing, hoping.

I reached for the knob, and—

as a huge crash of thunder shook the house and lit up the door floating above me—

I crumpled my hand against the cold wet wall and fell to the floor, moaning.

Sticky with fresh paint. Smeared now on my hand and forehead. I shook my hand and winced in pain. Had I broken a finger? I cradled my hand and felt like an idiot. *Of course* there was no knob to grasp. *Of course* there was no magic door in the wall. There was *never* a magic door, anywhere, ever. There was no such thing as magic, not in this world. Not for me and not for Jasper.

Then I heard a faint mew and turned to see Mr. Face's paws, scrambling for the slick window ledge across the room. I ran back to the window and reached over, scooped him up in my good left hand, thin and soaking.

But when I saw the mouse in his teeth, I screamed and dropped him again. He landed on his feet, glanced up at me, and laid the mouse neatly at my feet, next to my slippers on the little rag rug beside my bed. I shuddered. I stared at the little mouse, and Mr. Face stared up at me. Proud of himself.

I nudged the mouse with my foot. He didn't move.

Then I looked out, past the cat and the window and the porch. I stared out into the wind and the rain and the lightning and the trees moaning and bending and cracking in the night. The storm warned me. It cried danger.

But Jasper was there, trapped in that storm, alone.

So I climbed out into it.

REAL MAGIC

The real magic was that I could run.

Or the real magic was that I *decided* to.

I ran quickly, with the wet pavement shredding my bare feet and the rain beating hard on my head and back. I was soaked immediately, but I didn't slow down, or stop to rest, or glance around, even though my heart was pounding and the thunder was bursting and rolling and the lightning was splitting the sky above me. I ran.

Once I'd started, I don't think I could have slowed down. I couldn't have stopped, not even for a car, if I could have even heard it over the thunder and the rain. Something inside me, stronger than any logic, knew it needed to run. I dashed down to Hemlock and then up Berne and straight into the creek. I waded across as fast as I could. I couldn't see anything, and I stumbled over roots and rocks and jagged bits of bottle, but it was like I couldn't feel it, and my feet knew the way.

Then I was at the embankment, at the opening in the vines and brush, and I was grabbing for kudzu and pulling myself up the slippy rain-soaked hill, scrambling at the red clay incline, and I was falling, but climbing too, covered in scratches and brambles, plastered with mud.

At last, I could see the house in the darkness, with the faint glow from its windows. I stumbled and flailed as I dashed around the side of the building, made my way through the tall wet grass, and pushed at the door, which would not give. I banged at it. I pushed harder.

"Jasper!" I called.

Something was blocking my way, but I pushed and pushed, and at last, with a grating noise, the cinder blocks gave way, and the splintery old door let me in with a creak of hinges, and I burst into the room, breathless and shouting, "I'm here! I'm here!"

I looked around the dim room wildly for the man, for the danger, for Jasper. The wind outside shook the old loose panes of glass in the windows, and I could hear a steady drip somewhere in the darkness, even over the thunder all around us, but the room was mostly dry.

My eyes fell on the bed. There she was. Jasper sprawled

on her pile of sheets and blankets. She peered, squinting. She blinked at me, sleepy eyed.

"Leah? Is it morning?"

The lights along the floor cast a warm gleam on the blue blanket, and Jasper's tousled mop of hair was lopsided. She yawned as she smiled at me. She was calm. She was just like always. Jasper.

"I wasn't too late," I said. "You're okay."

"What do you mean?" A drop of rain plunked on her hand from a leak in the ceiling, and the crumbling house groaned with the wind. "What's wrong? Are you talking about the storm?"

I dropped to my knees beside her bed, panting, dripping. "Oh, God," I said. "I'm an idiot. There was nothing wrong. I imagined it."

"Leah, what's going on? Are you okay?" She looked worried.

Then it all hit me. My scraped feet and tired brain, my panting chest and the mud and rain soaking me. I toppled over onto the edge of her thin mattress. I looked like a freak and felt like a fool.

"I came . . . to help . . . you," I said, still trying to catch my breath. "I came . . . to make sure . . . you were safe."

Jasper laid a hand on my wet shoulder. She leaned over me and grinned into my face. "You're nice to worry," she said.

"A total weirdo for sure, and dripping water all over the parts of my bed that weren't already wet from the storm. But *very* nice."

I rolled off her blankets onto the floor. I tried to breathe like a normal person, whatever that meant.

Then, in the distance, somewhere near the house, I heard a shout.

"What was that?" said Jasper. Her eyes shot up to the window.

"I don't know," I whispered.

We sat in frozen silence for a moment, staring at each other. Waiting. Until we heard it again. A man's voice. Loud and angry. Bellowing in the rain. And then, at the padlocked front door, the sound of someone knocking. A fist, banging on wood.

"Oh no," I said. "It's *him*. That man."

Jasper's eyes were wide. "Who?"

"That guy," I said. "The one I told you about, with the tooth and the tattoos and the gun. He's here. I *knew* he would be. He saw the path to the Vine Realm!"

Jasper's eyes went wide. I nodded at her silently. We both waited, staring at each other. I counted the seconds. 1 . . . 2 . . . 3 . . . Until the sound came again.

BANG!

Only now he was at the back door, just behind my head,

here. He was here, and I hadn't even bothered to replace the cinder blocks when I came in.

"Oh, God," said Jasper.

BANG!

BANG! BANG!

The pounding shook the little house, rattled the windows and walls. And we sat frozen. There was nowhere to go. What could we do? Jasper reached for an empty root beer bottle and cocked it behind her head, as if she might throw it if someone tried to come in. We both stared at the door as the knob turned.

The rickety old door burst open with a crash that shook the room and shattered the cracked pane of glass all over us. Like diamonds, the shards twinkled everywhere. All across the floor, the bedding. Probably in my hair. I shook my head and looked up. My heart stopped pounding. My heart stopped. Or it felt that way.

A man stepped into the dimly lit room. He was tall and dripping wet and his eyes were wild.

"Leah!" he shouted.

A flashlight beam found me.

"Dad!" I cried.

The cold, white light found Jasper next, beside me on her mattress, huddled in her blue blanket.

"And you must be Jasper," said my dad. He tossed back

the hood of his raincoat and rubbed at his hair until it stood on end. Then he closed his eyes for a minute and just stood there above us. He was wearing his big black rainboots, but I saw that his old plaid pajamas were tucked inside them.

Jasper nodded. Bits of glass fell to the blanket. "Oh, Leah," she whispered, trembling. "What did you do?"

"I'm sorry," I said.

Then my dad opened his eyes, and I watched him take in everything as the flashlight beam darted around the room. Jasper, under the blanket I'd brought from our house. Mom's tablecloth. The sad assortment of cans and boxes that lined the counter. The bouquet of dead roses in their pickle jar. I saw it all through my father's eyes, and everything looked different.

Everything *was* different.

Of course, right about then, the storm died down. but even so, the walk home was unbearable. I almost would have welcomed thunder to drown out the silence. Nobody spoke as we left the house and trudged in the rain, slipping down the hill and then along the creek, following my dad and the sharp white beam of his flashlight. Jasper was behind me, gasping each time she tripped over something. Then we were out on the road, and we moved more quickly, though I was in no hurry to get home. I couldn't imagine what was about to happen. I couldn't even begin to guess.

At last we reached the house, where Mom was waiting for us on the porch, clutching a stack of soft dry towels. Dad went straight in the front door without even a word.

I looked up at the porch light. "The power's back on?" I said.

"Take your clothes off," Mom snapped in a neat, curt voice. As though she'd been rehearsing. She set the towels on the ground.

"Here?" I said. "No!"

"You will do as I say, Leah," she snapped. "You're covered in mud and soaked to the bone, and . . . is that glass in your hair?"

I nodded.

"Do it," she said. Then she turned and went inside.

I looked at Jasper. "I didn't tell them, I swear. He must have heard me, and followed. . . ."

But she just shook her head at me and turned away, raised her nightgown over her head. I turned around and did the same. Then I grabbed for one of the towels and wrapped it around myself. Silently, we walked into the living room, where Dad and Mom were waiting for us. Dad stood tall, with his arms crossed in front of him. His wet hair stood straight up, and he had changed into sweats and his threadbare blue robe. Mom was sitting in her old chair, rocking faintly, nervously.

Jasper glanced at me, as if waiting to see what I'd do, so I went first—across the room. I sat on the sofa. A moment

257

later, she joined me. Then for a while, we all just stared at each other.

At last, Mom stopped rocking and leaned forward. Her voice was surprisingly calm and kind when she asked, "What's going on here, girls?"

Jasper looked to me again. It was her story to tell, but her eyes were narrow slits, and they were my parents. I turned back to my mom. "It's hard to explain," I said. "I don't know what to say."

"Try," said Mom. "Try the truth."

My father cleared his throat. "They were in a vacant house, Rachel. Over near Red's Farm, back in the brambles. They had it set up like a playhouse. With a bed and everything."

My mom looked at me. "What?"

"It's nothing bad. We just had a hideout," I said. "A place of our own."

Mom shook her head. "That's a dangerous game, Leah. Anyone could be wandering around late at night, and nobody would hear you if you needed help. Dangerous people are out there, you know."

"I know!" I said. "That's why I went, to get Jasper. I was scared for her."

My mother's brow wrinkled. She turned to Jasper. "And where does your mom think you are tonight?"

Jasper only shrugged. At the other end of the couch, with

258

her hair wet and streaming down her back, she seemed smaller, somehow, and miles away.

"You'll find this will go much better if you answer her," said my dad. His voice was wound up tight, like it might explode.

"My . . ." Jasper stuttered. "My mother doesn't care where I am."

"Maybe it feels like that," said my mom. "But I'm certain that's not true."

Jasper laughed, but it wasn't a happy laugh. "I wish you were right, but you're not. My mom isn't like you. You wouldn't understand."

"It's true," I said, turning from my mom to my dad. "It's different for Jasper. Her mom isn't . . . around."

"Don't be ridiculous," said my mom, reaching into a pocket for her cell phone. "What's her number? It's time I talked to this woman."

"You can't," said Jasper simply. She didn't sound upset. She was just stating a fact. "Please. I won't bother Leah anymore. I won't ever come back here. I promise."

"No!" I cried.

"And so then what . . . ?" said my dad. "You'll go back to that shack? Soaking in your wet nightgown and flip-flops? Do you think we're going to let you do that?"

Jasper shrugged.

"No, seriously," he said. "What would you do, if you were us?"

Now all three of us were staring at Jasper. She was gazing at her feet, lost. The silence was unbearable.

At last, without lifting her head, she said, "I . . . I can't go back. To where I was living, before."

"Why not?" asked my mom. Her voice was soft but curious.

Jasper finally looked up at her, and her lip was trembling. "I can't tell you that. I want to . . . but I can't."

When Jasper said that, it was like something shifted inside Mom. But not in a bad way. Her face crumpled, and she rose and came over to the couch. She sat between us and put an arm around Jasper. Not me, but Jasper.

"Honey," she said, "whatever it is, I promise it's not as bad as you think. We can help. You just need to tell us. That's what we're here for."

Watching my mom hold Jasper, I felt slow soft tears in my eyes. She looked . . . like a mom. *My* mom. The real one. I had missed her so much. How I had missed her. I wanted to reach out for her myself in that moment, but it wasn't my turn. Jasper needed her now. I let my tears fall and then wiped their trails away.

Jasper shook her head. She still wasn't really crying, but her eyes shone too, and her voice was tight when she said, "People . . . say things like that. But it's just not true." She took a deep breath. "You can't help me. There's no way. If I thought you could, I would let you. I really would. That's all I want."

Then there was a sob, a wrenching sharp sound, almost a bark, and Jasper was crying.

Mom was still holding her, but she looked over at me now. I couldn't tell what she wanted me to say. I couldn't think of anything to say.

Across the room, Dad had uncrossed his arms. His brow was furrowed, and he strode toward us, to perch on the edge of the coffee table. His voice softened, but the words he spoke were terrible.

"Jasper, let us help you. I don't want to call the police, but if you don't tell us what's going on . . . that's what I'll have to do."

"No!" cried Jasper, through her tears.

"Then talk to us," said Dad. "Help us understand. We can't responsibly let you walk out into the street. How old are you, anyway?"

"Fourteen," said Jasper, sniffling.

"Yeah, see, you're just a kid. I would never be able to live with myself if I let you go. If you don't want to call your parents, I'll be forced to call the police."

"No," said Jasper, wiping her tears with her bare arm. "Please? Please don't do that?"

Everything was happening too fast, and I felt lost in it all. My parents were trying to help, and I knew it, but they didn't understand. And it was late at night, and they were tired and lost too, and I could see where this would end. It was a bad ending, but there was nothing I could do. Jasper was crying and Mom was crying, and my dad had his head in his hands now. They hadn't been able to handle the cat box for the last year or the lint trap. They hadn't been able to carry on a normal conversation, and now they were trying to handle this? They were broken. We were all broken. But somebody had to do something.

I opened my mouth, and when I spoke, it wasn't to my parents. It was to Jasper.

"That's it," I said. "It's over. You have to tell them. If you don't, I will."

"What?" Jasper looked up through her tears.

"They can't understand if you don't tell them," I said.

Mom was nodding, and Dad was nodding too.

"Leah," said Jasper. "You swore. You promised. . . ."

I nodded. "I know. But they're right. I figured that out tonight. I was so scared, Jasper. That man I saw, and the storm. I was so scared."

"I was *fine*," said Jasper.

"No," I said, "you really weren't, even if you thought that. This isn't a game. It isn't a playhouse, or a story. It's real. And even if you hate me forever now, I know it's true. We can't handle this on our own. And something bad will happen eventually, even if you manage to run back to the Vine Realm, or somewhere else like it. And I'll have to live with just standing by, letting it happen. You *have* to tell them, or I will."

Jasper shook her head.

So I took a deep breath, and it felt like something was tearing inside me, but I couldn't look away from the truth. I couldn't just sit there on the raft and survive alone while she sank beneath whatever it was that might drown her.

"Jasper's mom is gone," I said. "She's not around. She's . . . bad news."

"Oh, sweetheart," said Mom, looking at Jasper. "What kind of—"

"It doesn't matter right now," I said, and Mom broke off midsentence.

My parents were still listening, but I couldn't look at them, because there was fury in Jasper's eyes. I could see it. Her jaw was set and she looked like she was ready to stand up, kick open the door, and run off and never look back. But I kept going.

"So she's supposed to be living with her sister, in East Lake. But her sister's husband—he's . . . bad news too."

"What kind of bad news?" asked Dad.

Jasper was shaking her head, staring at me. "You *promised*," she said. "You're supposed to be my best friend."

"I *am* your best friend," I said. "Or I'm trying to be." I

turned back to my parents. "He's bad, like . . . *physical*. Violent. And when Jasper told her sister to leave him, her sister said no. She's afraid she'll lose her kids. It's complicated. So she gave Jasper some money, and Jasper left. She checks in sometimes."

Mom and Dad were having a silent conversation with their eyes. I couldn't figure out what they were saying, but it looked serious.

At last, Mom said, "Okay. Well. I think maybe this is more than we can handle tonight. How about we all need to get a good night's sleep and discuss this in the morning?"

Dad nodded. "I think that's the right idea. And just in case anyone gets any funny ideas, you girls should both know, if anyone leaves in the night, I'll call the police. Right away. End of story. Am I understood?"

Jasper and I both nodded.

Somehow, we all went to bed after that, like it was a normal night. We took quick showers, brushed our teeth, and crawled under our covers. Me in my bed, and Jasper on the floor in a sleeping bag and a borrowed nightgown.

"Good night," I whispered.

Jasper didn't reply. She just turned away from me.

I lay there in the darkness, staring at her unforgiving back, feeling like we'd come to a wall at the end of a very dark hallway. But then I happened to glance down at the rag rug next to her pillow. And I remembered the mouse.

"Where'd you go?" I whispered. I sat up and peered at the floor around the rug, at the spot where, a few hours earlier, a tiny body had been laid. But the mouse was gone. There was no sign of him at all.

I closed my eyes and slept.

CONVERSATION O'CLOCK

When I woke, it was to the sound of Jasper snoring lightly on the floor beside me. She was curled up into a tiny ball and had sort of wiggled her way over toward my bed in the night, so that she was sleeping almost directly beneath me. I peered down at her and noticed for the first time that her lashes weren't brown but a deep dark red. I lay there like that for a minute, watching her snore. She seemed so calm, so at home, curled safely in my room. But watching her put an ache in my belly. What would happen to her? I didn't want her to wake up. I wanted her to sleep on and on. I wondered what she was dreaming about.

It was still really early. Outside the window, it was almost dark, but I could hear birds. I slipped carefully out of bed and stepped over my sleeping friend. Then I crept across the room. And out in the hallway, I did something I hadn't done in over a year: I made my way down the hall to my parents' room, where I knocked lightly on the door and then went in.

They were sleeping on opposite sides of the bed, as far from each other as possible. Mom had fallen asleep with her small reading lamp on, and her book had dropped to the floor beside her. Dad had his face tucked down, under the covers, but I could see the top of his head, where the hair was thinning. They faced away from each other.

Without stopping to think about it, I climbed up at the foot of the bed and slid in between them, into the narrow valley between their sleeping backs. I hadn't done it in a long time, and I could feel how much bigger I was than the last time I'd tried to crawl between them. But somehow I fitted myself into the space, the same one Sam and I both crammed into on Sunday mornings. It felt good and snug. I wriggled a little, hoping they'd wake up.

When they didn't stir, I turned to my mom's sleeping back. "Rise and shine," I whispered in her ear.

"Huh?" Slowly, Mom turned over and forced her eyes open. It took her a second of blinking to really see me. When she did, she sat up right away. "Leah? Is everything okay?"

I shook my head. "Of course not," I said. "Can we please talk?"

Mom sank back against the headboard, back against her

pillow, sighed, and reached for the glass of water by her bed. "Sure we can. Just give me a second. I'm not really awake yet." She took a sip of water, a long slow swallow, and then shook her head. "Last night feels like a terrible dream. Where's Jasper now?"

"Still sleeping."

"Good," said Mom gently.

"I didn't want to wake her," I said, "because I wanted to talk to you *about* her."

Mom reached over across me and poked my dad in the back. "Paul," she said. "Paul, wake up."

He grunted in reply, and flopped over to face us, but his eyes were still closed. "Uhhhh," he said. "What time is it?"

"Time to get up," said Mom. "Conversation o'clock."

He opened one eye.

"Your delinquent daughter wants to talk to you, and I think we should listen. Rouse thyself."

Dad sat up and scratched his head. He looked down at me, lying there next to Mom. "Okay, let me have it, delinquent daughter."

It was funny that, as terrible as the situation was, things felt better between us than they had in a year. As if a rubber band that had been stretching tighter and tighter every day had suddenly snapped and broken and all the tension was gone now.

I took a deep breath and sat up, then repositioned myself in the middle of the bed, so that I could look at both of them at once. "Okay!" I said. "I know I have gotten in all kinds of trouble lately. I've done a lot of things wrong. And, yeah, I probably deserve to be grounded—"

"*I'm* nearly certain of it," said Dad.

"Hush!" said Mom. "*Leah's* turn."

"The thing is," I continued, "that stuff is all about *me, my* mistakes. And I want to talk to you guys about Jasper, not me. Because she hasn't done *anything* wrong. So can we hold off on me and just focus on her right now?"

"We can try that, Leah," said Mom. "We can *try*. Jasper seems like a nice kid. She really does. She has a sort of glow, doesn't she?"

"She does!" I blurted out gratefully. "She *totally* does. Honestly, I don't understand how someone so great came out of something so terrible. It's like she hasn't had any chance to be happy, but somehow she knows how to do it anyway. It's like she's so full of joy, nothing can squish it."

Mom didn't say anything, just nodded.

"So that's why we have to help her. Obviously, she can't stay where she's living any longer, or move back with her mom, but . . ."

Dad raised a hand. "Now, hold your horses, Leah," he said. "We don't even know what we're dealing with. What exactly is her story? Even if what you told us is true, what about her dad? Her grandparents? Someone?"

"There are people," I admitted, "but they just aren't *there*.

She's never met her dad, and her mom drinks a lot and got in trouble for drunk driving and other stuff, so they took Jasper away to go live with her sister, but, like we told you last night, her sister's husband . . . he hits her. I didn't ask about more than that." I took a breath. "You can ask Jasper, I guess. If you really want to. I'm not sure how much she'll tell you. She's pretty scared."

"Poor girl," said Mom. She reached out to me and squeezed my knee.

"That's terrible . . . if it's true," said Dad slowly.

"Of course it's *true!*" I said. "Why would she lie? Why would she run away if it wasn't true?"

Dad shook his head. "People do all kinds of strange things, Leah. You're too young to really know that. But—"

I sat up straight. "Jasper's not a liar!" I said firmly.

"In any case," said Dad, "something's very wrong in her life. And I feel bad for her. I just don't know what we can really do. I mean, you can be her friend, of course, no matter what happens. And maybe if she needs a lawyer, we could help her financially. That might make a difference. But—"

"No. I don't mean lawyers. I mean, can *we* help her? Just help her ourselves? Like I've been doing?"

Mom shook her head. "Honey, I know this is hard for you to understand. But sometimes, there are problems that aren't ours to solve. That are simply too big for us to fix. Sometimes it's better not to help someone. . . ."

"Better not to help someone?" I repeated slowly. "Is that what you just said?"

Mom frowned and pulled her knees up under the covers, hugged them close. "That isn't what I meant to say," she said. "I only meant . . ."

I could feel myself getting upset, but I wanted to stay calm. I wanted them to hear me. "But don't you get it, Mom? She's living in an abandoned house with no running water or electricity, because that's better than home. She has *nobody*. Truly nobody. Except . . . maybe me."

"Leah," said Dad, "I love that you want to help. But you're a kid. And I think what your mom means is that there are people trained for this kind of thing. There are therapists and social workers. The responsible thing to do is to call those people."

"I *knew* you'd say that," I said. "I just knew you would. That's the *Dad* answer. But this time you're wrong."

Dad shook his head. "I don't see what we can do for her. We have no place in this whole mess. We don't know this girl, this family. We're strangers, Leah."

I looked up at my dad then, and I felt . . . disappointed.

"You're only strangers if you choose to be strangers," I said. "A few weeks ago, Jasper and I were strangers, and then we chose each other. *You* can choose too."

My dad looked at me and held his hands up, as if to show me they were empty.

"*This* is exactly why Jasper was keeping secrets," I continued. "*This* is what she was afraid of. She'd rather be alone in a storm than go wherever we'd send her."

"Sometimes we have to do things that people don't like, because it's what's best. That's what it means, to be a grown-up.

I shook my head again. "And when we go to visit her at some group home, or something . . . and if she's miserable, will you still think it was for the best? Because it'll be *your fault.* For sending her away."

Mom frowned slightly at that. "Even so . . . ," she said. Then she paused and chewed at her lip. Which meant she was confused.

I watched her closely, and then I just said it. "Jasper should live *here.* With us."

"Nope," said Dad, practically before the words were even out of my mouth. "No way."

"But why? "

"It's just not possible," he said.

Mom was frowning at Dad across the bed. "I think . . . I think what your father means to say is that as much as we'd love to take her in, it just won't work." She shook her head. "I want you to know I really am hearing you. I get that this is terrible. And I know why you feel the way you do. I can conjure up that guilt so clearly. How we'll feel if this all ends badly.

Do you think I don't wake up every day thinking about how we sent *him* . . . your brother . . . off to camp, when he didn't want to go?"

"Wait, what?" I said.

"Of course I'd love to just say, well, let's just ignore everything and take Jasper in and nothing will ever hurt her again!" she went on. "But that's a solution from a storybook. A happily-ever-after. She's not a stray kitten, Leah. You can't adopt a kid, just like that."

"Why not?"

"Well, because she has her own family," said Mom. "We can't know what her sister is feeling right now. She might be panic-stricken. And her mom could be in rehab this minute."

"Okay fine," I said. "But what if she isn't? I mean, her sister is right there down the street in East Lake. Jasper's been checking in regularly, and nobody even brought her food or anything."

"Really?" said Mom. She was chewing her lip again. Now she crossed her arms tightly. "That just seems . . . hard to believe."

"Yeah, well, it's the truth. So what if her sister *doesn't* care? Or what if she cares, but can't deal with it for . . . other reasons. What if they make her live with her sister's bad-news husband, and he hits her? Doesn't that seem likely? What happens *then*?"

"Then . . . I guess she'll go into foster care for a few years," said Mom. "And I know that doesn't sound ideal, but it doesn't have to be bad. Look at what happened to Seth Jones, from your class in school—"

"Not *ideal*?" I said. "How would you feel if *I* went to foster care?"

"Don't be ridiculous," Dad broke in. "That would never happen. You'd go to your grandparents."

"So what if her sister says it's okay?" I asked. "Then can she live here? Can *we* be her foster family?"

"We *have* a family, Leah," said Mom. "We can't just add a stranger into the mix here. We're busy and distracted and limited already. The last year has been . . ."

"Horrible!" I said. "It's been horrible and depressing."

"Yes," said Dad. "Exactly. So do you think we're really equipped to take on an extra kid? Is that fair to Jasper?"

"Fair to Jasper?"

Dad nodded. "Fair to Jasper. To take her in when we're . . ." He trailed off.

"That's a trash reason." I sneered. I couldn't help it. "That's some grown-up excuse for something you don't want to do. It doesn't even mean anything, and you know it. She'd *way* rather be here. She was just saying how great she thought Mom was."

"Really?" said Mom with a small smile.

I looked from Dad to Mom. "Come on, please? Mom? Dad? Can't you please wake up and realize I'm right this time? I really *am* right!"

It was true, and I knew it. Maybe magic wasn't real, but *this* was the next best thing. So obvious. So easy. It was so close, right *there*. I could see a sunnier version of all our futures peeking out. I could taste something sweet.

Mom sighed. "Look, Leah, I'm going to be honest. As much as I get what you're saying, your dad is right. We've been running on fumes. Even if Jasper's sister said yes, and the social services people said it was okay and everything . . . I just . . . I can't do more than I'm doing right now. Heck, I can't even seem to buy laundry detergent. Some days, I lose track of what time it is. I manage to make a real dinner once a week, at best. I can't take in an extra kid. I'm barely hanging on. Can't you see that? We've been . . . struggling. You know it's true."

"I know," I said. "But haven't you noticed things have been . . . better? With Jasper? I haven't been so . . . lonely. Or empty. She's not extra work. She's like . . . sunshine. Or vitamins, or a circus, or something . . ."

Unbelievably, Mom seemed to be listening seriously now. She nodded slowly at me. "Actually, yes, I did notice," she said. "When she was here the other day, I felt . . . different. It was like we'd opened up a bunch of windows in the house."

"See?" I said.

"But that was for a day, Leah. Not a lifetime. Not when she gets into fights at school or starts dating some horrible boy or something. I won't be able to cope."

"Well, if you say she can live with us, *I* promise not to date

275

horrible boys. How's that? Jasper can be the difficult one, and I'll be the best kid ever."

"Now you're just being silly," said Mom. "Of course Jasper is welcome to visit anytime. Like any friend of yours. No matter where she's living. But people don't just decide to adopt a fourteen-year-old."

"Some people do! Mother Teresa took in a whole orphanage. We studied her in school."

"I'm hardly Mother Teresa," said Mom. "Most people aren't. It's just not something normal people do."

"Something normal people do . . . ," I repeated under my breath. "*That's* a laugh."

"What do you mean by *that*?" asked Dad. He'd mostly just been sitting there, listening, but he was starting to get angry now, wearing out. I could tell. He was rubbing his forehead in a headachy way.

"Honestly? I don't care about *what normal people do* anymore," I said. "I don't want things to be *normal*. Not if *normal* is what we've been doing for the last year. Normal is depressing. It's pretending."

"Isn't that a little melodramatic?" said Dad.

I shook my head. "No! Ever since Sam died, it's like none of us are really *here*. You guys are so . . . Well, Dad, all you do is stare into your phone all day, every day. And then pretend to play darts and go out to the garage and sit alone there, with your weird painting."

Dad's mouth opened and closed a few times, but no words came out.

"What painting?" Mom said.

"See!" I said. "Mom, you didn't even know. Dad's been painting a mural on the ceiling in the garage for, like, months now! Is that *normal*?"

"Really?" She turned to Dad. "What's she talking about? A mural of what?"

But I wasn't done. "Both of you . . . I'm not *blaming* you, exactly. I know you're sad. But it makes things worse for me. Mom looks like . . ." I looked at her. "Like she's going to break into pieces half the time."

Mom nodded. And all she said was "It's been hard."

"I know it," I said. "And until Jasper, I just sort of accepted that this was how things were going to be from now on. Hard and sad. But when I met her, it was like I got a do-over. I remembered how to laugh and tell people things. And I realized it's not okay. The last year has *not* been okay. I have been *so* lonely," I said, and I wasn't ready to stop talking yet, but a sob snuck out and interrupted me.

"You're right, Leah," Dad said quietly. "We have a lot of fixing to do."

"We're trying," Mom added. "We really are. And I think we're getting better, a little. . . ."

I took a deep breath and forced myself to continue. "Until I met Jasper, I thought I was broken for good. I didn't seem to be able to talk to anyone anymore, and I thought I wouldn't ever be happy again, because of Sam. Because it was my fault that he . . ."

"Oh, honey," said Mom.

"But then I realized I wasn't broken for good. It was like magic. How being with Jasper sort of fixed me. Woke me back up. But it isn't just me. It's *all* of us. It's like . . . like we were your coffee cup, the four of us, and the cup could hold joy and fun and *everything*. But when Sam died, that cracked the cup. So now it doesn't hold anything anymore. We try to put things in it. But everything just . . . dribbles out."

"Oh, Leah, no," said Mom. She looked like she might cry too.

I nodded. "Yes! And now Jasper is here, and she's not taking Sam's place, exactly. But she's patching the cup. She's the glue. I know the crack won't go away, ever. We can't pretend the cup wasn't broken. But we can fill it again. Can't we?"

"That's a very wise thing you just said," said Mom. "A wise thing . . ."

"Well, maybe if I'm so wise, you should listen to me," I insisted.

Dad took a moment before speaking again. "Leah, even if we wanted to, I don't know how it would work, legally. We might have to go to court. It's just not a thing people do, to take in some kid off the street."

"Then I don't want to do *what people do*," I said. "I want to invent our own way to do things. Maybe she can just have an overnight here, like Tess used to. And then she can have an overnight tomorrow, and the night after that, and the night after that. I bet her sister would let her. It's better than living on the streets."

Dad didn't say anything, and I knew that meant I was right. But Mom sighed. "You're going to discover, Leah, that the world is full of sad people, sick people, people with problems. You can't fix everyone. And it isn't your fault when you can't."

"I know that, Mom," I said. "But I'm not trying to *fix* Jasper. Aren't you listening to me? We have a room that is just sitting there, empty. That room hurts. It's not a memory. It's a hole. And meanwhile, we have this person who could fill it, a person who's all alone."

"It's true," said Dad slowly. "That room . . . it's . . ."

I waited. To see what he'd say. But he only put one hand over his eyes and fell silent again.

"No!" I said. "Stop it! It's too much. The sadness is too much." I reached up and pulled his hand down, held it. "No more sadness, not like that. Sam is gone and that room is a dusty, horrible shrine. So why not?" I said. "Why not Jasper?"

Mom was staring at me now. "Leah," she said. "What happened to your brother—"

279

"Sam," I said. I was done with Mom not being able to say his name. "You mean *Sam*."

"Yes," said Mom. "What happened to . . . Sam . . ."

"Yeah?"

"You can't go back and fix it. You can't change what's already past."

I rose to my knees on the bed. "I *know* that," I said. I was ready to scream. I felt like they weren't hearing anything I said. "But I'm not trying to change the past. I'm trying to change the present. For all of us. All you have to do is say yes. You *can* say yes. It's like . . . an actual magic word."

Then we heard a cough, and we all turned together to find Jasper standing in the doorway in my blue flowered nightgown.

"Hi," she said matter-of-factly. She looked different somehow, younger than usual, though her legs were too long for the nightgown.

"Hello," Dad replied awkwardly, with a little wave.

"I rolled up the sleeping bag," said Jasper. "And I wondered where you wanted me to put it."

She sounded brave to me. She sounded like herself. Like a girl who is going to do a hard thing, and is used to doing hard things. But then she put her hands on her hips awkwardly, like she wasn't sure what to do with them.

She was scared.

All around me then, there was a pause. It was like the whole room held its breath. An unbearably long breath. I glanced back and saw that my parents were staring at each other.

"Please?" I whispered. My voice was shaky in my throat. "Please?"

My dad reached out, put a hand on my back. "I'm sorry," he whispered.

In the doorway, Jasper shifted from foot to foot.

Then, out of nowhere, my mom suddenly said, "Huh!" Like she'd had a new thought.

"Rach?" asked my dad.

She turned to him and locked eyes. "Paul," she said. "Do you remember what you told me when I was scared we weren't ready to get married, but you wanted to run off to Vegas?"

Dad's eyes softened, but they were still fixed on Mom. His voice was low when he said, "I told you we could handle anything if we were together."

"That's right," said Mom. And it was funny because the moment felt sort of romantic, but her voice was sharp, like she was on a phone call for work. "You weren't afraid of risks back then. Or messes. You used to throw whole buckets of paint at a canvas and tell me we could worry about the floor later, remember that? You used to take me on road trips without a map or a destination. You used to do all kinds of crazy things. Remember?"

Dad nodded. "I do," he said. "And then there was that night on the mountain above Chattanooga . . ." He grinned at her.

Mom blushed.

I didn't say a word. I had said all my words, maybe too many. I knew it wasn't my turn anymore. So I just watched them stare at each other and wondered what had happened on that mountain. I didn't think I'd ever know. I probably didn't *want* to know.

"The thing is," said Mom, "we have done the hardest thing we will ever do, haven't we? What happened last summer— nothing else will ever be anything like that. So we know you were right. We *can* do anything, together. Anything at all."

Dad nodded.

All this time Jasper had just been standing there, not saying a word. Watching the story unfold, like we were a play on a stage. Now I looked up at her and tried to make eye contact, but she didn't seem to notice me. She was set on my mom. Her eyes almost seemed glazed over. I wondered what she was thinking. What she was seeing.

This is a family, I thought to myself.

This is people, not ghosts.

This is us, waking up, no matter what happens next. . . .

Since nobody was paying attention to me, I closed my eyes.

I crossed my fingers.

I held my breath and wished.

When I opened my eyes again, I saw that Mom and Dad had broken their gaze. Mom was glancing briefly around the room, as if taking it all in—the sunlight, the rumpled blankets, the water in its glass on the bedside table. But Dad was looking straight out into the doorway, at Jasper.

"Please?" I whispered one last time.

Dad coughed. "I wonder, Jasper—how do you like your eggs?"

But Mom pulled up her knees under the covers and patted the empty spot on the bed in front of her. "Come on in," she said. "Let's talk."

"Really?" said Jasper as she stepped forward into the room. "What about?"

Mom nodded. "It seems we're having a family meeting," she said. "You should probably join us."

LIKE ANY OTHER DAY

I was sprawled on the porch, elbows deep in pumpkin guts, when the screen door slammed and I looked up to see my mom, holding out two cans of fizzy water. "I thought you girls might like a cold drink," she said. "Awfully warm for October. Doesn't really feel like Halloween, does it?"

I shook my head and withdrew my hands, scooping out gobs of slimy seeds, and tossed the mess down with a splat on the newspapers spread around me. "Not even a little bit," I grumbled.

Across from me, Jasper called out, "Thanks, Rachel! Can I have the lime?"

"No fair," I said, wiping my hands on my jeans. "Lime's my favorite."

"Sorry, kid," said Mom as she passed a green can to Jasper and set the cranberry water by my pumpkin. Then she leaned over to look at our pumpkins, frowned, and added, "Wow, these jack-o'-lanterns are going to be quite . . . interesting."

"What do you mean?" I asked, leaning back to examine my own pumpkin, on which I'd scribbled in black marker the outline of where I was about to start cutting. Three triangles and a toothy grin, just like every other year. "His name is Shady McPumpkinhead," I said.

"Of *course* it is," said Mom. "Of the Tennessee McPumpkinheads, yes?"

I glanced over at Jasper's pumpkin, which was already finished. I had no idea what it was supposed to be. "Where's his nose?" I asked, tilting my head sideways for a different angle. "And . . . the rest of his face?"

Jasper tilted her head too. "What makes you assume it's a boy pumpkin?" she asked.

I shrugged. "The patriarchy, probably."

Jasper laughed. "Look, I refuse to be boxed in by your conventional holiday customs," she said. "*My* jack-o'-lantern is an abstract expression of autumn."

"A protest pumpkin, eh?" said Mom.

Jasper nodded. "Why not?"

"No reason," said Mom, turning. "*You* rage against the machine all you want. I'm going inside to start dinner. We're having garlic chicken."

The minute she was gone, Jasper grinned and whispered at me, "Garlic chicken with extra garlic!"

"Don't say I never warned you!"

"Truth!" said Jasper, cracking open her fizzy water.

I picked up my knife and stared at my pumpkin, trying to decide where to start cutting. "I can't wait for you to see Halloween in Ormewood," I said. "Trick-or-treating on Woodland is like nothing you've ever experienced. It's almost a festival. They block the street off and literally *thousands* of kids show up."

"*Literally* thousands?"

"No, I really mean it. Literally *literally*. Like, *actually* thousands. Andy, around the corner, keeps track each year of how much candy he gives out. Last year he ran out after twelve hundred pieces."

"You don't say . . . ," said Jasper. Then she seemed to drift off a little, like she was thinking about something.

"I *do* say," I insisted, and shoved the knife into Shady McPumpkinhead's face, chopped out an eye with three quick movements.

Then Jasper cleared her throat and said, "Hey . . . Leah?"

I looked up. "Yeah?"

"Well," she said. "It's just . . . I was thinking that maybe I could . . . invite my sister to come over, bring her kids to trick-or-treat. What do you think?"

"Oh!" I said, laying down my knife. "That . . . would be

awesome. I bet Dad would make some of his special apple cider soda, and—"

Jasper rolled her eyes. "Be real, Leah," she said. "It will *not* be awesome. It's almost certain to be awkward. But I miss her, and I was thinking how it's strange you haven't met her yet. So I thought . . . maybe it was a good time. And the kids will have a blast. If it's like you say, a festival?"

The truth was that sometimes I managed to forget all about Jasper's family. She'd slid so neatly into our house that it was easy to avoid thinking about all the hard stuff. The same way I could sometimes now, for a little while, avoid thinking about Sam. My brain got full of homework and chores and other things. I'd laugh and talk and be distracted for hours at a time. And then, in bed at night, Sam would come back with a whoosh. Like he was sitting there on the foot of my bed, waiting for me when the lights went out. Sometimes at night I still cried, alone. But I knew how to play the sad game now. And my therapist said that was a fine thing to do. I wondered if Jasper cried too, when she was alone. Maybe in the shower, where we couldn't hear her over the water.

Anyway, of *course* Jasper's sister should come over for Halloween. And maybe her mom too. I knew she talked to them both, and that things were a little better. But she hadn't really told me much about any of that. And I didn't ask. I figured Mom and Dad were involved. Some days the three of them got into the car and were gone for a few hours, and I knew that was how it should be. I trusted that things were okay. Or at least they were better. It was nice, after a summer of carrying secrets, to let someone else guard them for a while. To trust. I felt lighter.

Jasper started messing around with her phone then, texting someone really fast, so I took a sip of my soda and turned my attention back to Shady McPumpkinhead. Nobody said anything for a few minutes. I finished carving his mouth and decided to give him some ears.

But suddenly I heard Jasper say, "Ew, gross!" and I looked up from my jack-o'-lantern, to see that Mr. Face had silently joined us on the porch. He was sitting politely on the mat, a mouse between his teeth.

"Oh!" I said.

He held the creature delicately, like always. Only this time, since I was sitting on the ground, he was basically at eye level. After a moment, he turned his head, to look at Jasper the same way. Then, ever so gently, he laid his precious bundle on the mat, turned, and ran off.

Jasper shuddered. "Ugh, trick or treat, Mr. Face!" she said as she stretched a long leg, to nudge at the mouse with her foot, kick him off the porch.

But I reached out and grabbed her leg, stopped her. "No, wait," I said.

"Why?" she said. "It's gross."

"Just because," I said. "I know it seems gross, but it's not. I don't think so, anyway. Just wait. And watch."

"Watch *what?*" she asked, staring at me, baffled. "A dead mouse?"

"You'll see," I said.

And then the little brown mouse slowly uncurled himself, like I knew he would. He sat up on his haunches and gave a quick shake, as if waking from a nap. He brushed his whiskers lightly with his paws, and then he peered up at each of us briefly before he scampered off the mat, across the porch, down the stairs, and into the azaleas. We followed him with our eyes until he was gone.

Jasper shook her head. "Whoa. Did you see that?"

"I know," I said.

"How did you know that was going to happen?"

"I've seen it before," I said.

Jasper's eyes were wide. "Seriously?" she said. "That's more than weird. That's . . . impossible. It's like . . . actual magic. I almost don't believe it happened."

"Maybe it *is* magic," I said. "Or maybe he's just a really lucky mouse. You know, it's funny, how once you see something unbelievable happen a few times, it stops being so unbelievable."

Jasper didn't answer me. She just sat there for a second, holding her can of soda, and for once I couldn't read her face.

She looked thoughtful. I wondered what she was thinking, sitting like that for so long.

"*What?*" I said finally. "What is it?"

Jasper shook her head gently. "Nothing," she said. "Or . . . not *nothing*. I just—I feel lucky. You know?"

I nodded. I smiled. "I *do* know," I said. And that was true.

Jasper pushed herself up to standing. "You know what would make this day absolutely perfect?"

"Tell me."

"Ice cream!" she said.

"Oh, indeed!" I replied. "Ice cream is the best idea!" And it was. Ice cream suddenly sounded just right. It was still hot in the sunshine. "Maybe we could share a banana split."

"Perfect!"

Then Jasper reached down a hand to me, and I grabbed on. She pulled me up, and we ran inside to wash our hands. In no time at all, we were back on the porch, with the screen door slamming. We took off down the steps and headed for Morelli's and a banana split to share.

Just like on any other day, we shuffled through the dry leaves and faded grass of autumn. Just like on any other day, we talked and laughed as we hurried along. Just like on any other day, the sky was big and blue above us, and the pavement was cracked beneath our feet. All around us, the world was full of things—lights and shadows and air and wind and noises and cars moving and trees growing and kudzu vining and cats pouncing and everyone living their lives. The world was so big and so full, and that was just fine.

But most of it didn't concern us.

Not me and Jasper.

Not right now.

ACKNOWLEDGMENTS

When I was eight, my cousin Scott died. We weren't terribly close, but we were exactly the same age, and his death was a huge shock to me. It was my first encounter with the death of a child—always a terrible disruption in the order of things. I was frightened and confused. I had so many questions, but what I quickly discovered was that nobody could (or would) answer them.

A few years later, when I was about Jasper's age, I discovered that I had several friends who were living on their own, without parents. Somehow, they were feeding themselves, keeping their houses (mostly) clean, and managing to get to school. As shocking as that was, I never considered reporting any of these situations to an adult. The kid code was clear to me—even when I was concerned for my friends, my job was to keep quiet, and show up with groceries or petty cash when I could.

I'm still not exactly sure why these two sets of memories converged as they did in *My Jasper June*. I know that I wanted to write about the dangers of silence and the secrets kids keep. I wanted to write about pain and how friendship—*real* friendship—can ease that pain. Above all, I wanted to write about how strong kids can be, and about how grown-ups often underestimate their experiences. I wanted to tell a story about how sometimes kids step in and do the work their parents can't, for each other. And, in doing so, create their own chosen families.

This book went through many drafts and incarnations, and I had to dwell in some dark memories to write it. While I don't want to reveal anything identifiable about people who value their privacy, I need to acknowledge them here. I'm so thankful to the friends I had in those years—the kids who opened their lives and homes to me when we were young. Who made themselves vulnerable, and taught me to do the same. Life wasn't always pretty as we fumbled along together, but we made it through (on a steady diet of ramen), and I'm very grateful to those folks. I hope they know what they meant to me.

Of course, I need to thank a million other people. I'm indebted to my family of origin, and my kids, as always. But especially, for this particular book, I want to thank my chosen family. Most of all my husband, Chris Poma, and my best friend, Susan Gray. I don't know who I'd be without the two of you.

I want to thank the families I was lucky enough to find in Chattanooga and Iowa City, so many years ago—roommates and coworkers, musicians and writers. And more recently in Atlanta—my Ormewood Park neighbors, our ANCS school community, Congregation Bet Haverim, and the Atlanta Havurah. As well as the family of friends who support me daily, especially the women of the LSG, the Hamline MFAC program, and the small circle of other writers who read for me, share, and listen. I've decided not to try to name everyone here. There are just too many people who matter, and I live in fear of leaving someone out. But I hope you all know who you are.

I'd like to thank AIR Serenbe for granting me a generous Mulberry Street Focus Fellowship, and the gift of time and silence in a beautiful place.

Naturally, I need to thank everyone at Walden Pond Press and HarperCollins, the folks who helped me make this book. Especially Jordan Brown, an editor who sees what I mean to say before I do, and Debbie Kovacs, who is an actual fairy godmother. Special thanks to Ramona Kaulitzki for a cover that captures both the dazzle and the shadow of being thirteen. And much gratitude to Sylvie Shaffer, for reading with kind and honest eyes.

Lastly, I need to thank Tina Dubois—my agent and dear friend. Five years ago, when I first attempted to write this book, Tina was incredibly honest with me about what I needed to do. I wasn't able to handle her advice at that time, and I set the book aside. But when—years later—I felt up to the task, it was Tina's patience and startling intelligence that made it possible to reimagine this story. To make it what it needed to be. I couldn't do this job without her.